MW01340632

The CHRISTMAS HOUSE

BOOKS BY BEVERLY LEWIS

The Christmas House
The Heirloom
The Orchard
The Beginning
The Stone Wall
The Tinderbox
The Timepiece
The First Love
The Road Home
The Proving
The Ebb Tide
The Wish
The Atonement
The Photograph
The Love Letters
The River

HOME TO HICKORY HOLLOW

The Fiddler
The Bridesmaid
The Guardian
The Secret Keeper
The Last Bride

THE ROSE TRILOGY

The Thorn
The Judgment
The Mercy

ABRAM'S DAUGHTERS

The Covenant
The Betrayal
The Sacrifice
The Prodigal
The Revelation

THE HERITAGE OF LANCASTER COUNTY

The Shunning
The Confession
The Reckoning

ANNIE'S PEOPLE

The Preacher's Daughter
The Englisher
The Brethren

THE COURTSHIP OF NELLIE FISHER

The Parting
The Forbidden
The Longing

SEASONS OF GRACE

The Secret
The Missing
The Telling
The Postcard
The Crossroad

The Redemption of Sarah Cain
Sanctuary
(with David Lewis)
Child of Mine
(with David Lewis)
The Sunroom
October Song
Beverly Lewis Amish Romance Collection

Amish Prayers
The Beverly Lewis Amish Heritage Cookbook, 20th Anniversary Edition

BeverlyLewis.com

The Christmas House

An Amish Christmas Novella

Beverly Lewis

BethanyHouse
a division of Baker Publishing Group
Minneapolis, Minnesota

Published by Bethany House Publishers
Minneapolis, Minnesota
BethanyHouse.com

Bethany House Publishers is a division of
Baker Publishing Group, Grand Rapids, Michigan

Printed in the United States of America

Library of Congress Cataloging-in-Publication Data
Names: Lewis, Beverly, author.
Title: The Christmas house : an Amish Christmas novella / Beverly Lewis.
Description: Minneapolis, Minnesota : Bethany House Publishers, a division of Baker Publishing Group, 2025.
Identifiers: LCCN 2024054644 | ISBN 9780764244681 (cloth) | ISBN 9781493451272 (ebook)
Subjects: LCSH: Amish—Fiction. | LCGFT: Christmas fiction. | Christian fiction. | Novellas.
Classification: LCC PS3562.E9383 C57 2025 | DDC 813/.54—dc23/eng/20241122
LC record available at https://lccn.loc.gov/2024054644

Unless otherwise indicated, Scripture quotations are from the King James Version of the Bible.

Cover design and photography by Design Source Creative Services, Dan Thornberg

Baker Publishing Group publications use paper produced from sustainable forestry practices and postconsumer waste whenever possible.

25 26 27 28 29 30 31 7 6 5 4 3 2 1

To my readers who requested
a Hickory Hollow Christmas story.

"Christmas! 'Tis the season for kindling the fire of hospitality in the hall, the genial flame of charity in the heart."

—Washington Irving

1

Signs of the Christmas season were visible all over Lancaster County, Pennsylvania, even this early in November. Vendors at the local farmers markets had put out homemade candy canes, snowman-shaped chocolates, and chunks of fudge wrapped in cellophane and red bows. Many of the big chain stores had been displaying artificial trees, lights, and ornaments for a while now, nudging shoppers into the spirit of giving.

The signs were less noticeable in Hickory Hollow's strict Amish community, though. Oh, there were a few battery-operated candles already twinkling in young Amish couples' front windows, and in *all* of Ella Mae Zook's windows, upstairs and down. She had even boldly decorated her front door with a simple evergreen wreath, but then, the elderly widow was known to march to the beat of her own drum.

Otherwise, things in the secluded farming community looked much as they did any other late autumn day during wedding season. On nearly every road come Tuesdays and Thursdays in November and much of December, there were numerous horse-drawn carriages, as well as large church wagons filled with wooden benches and boxes of tableware, headed to various brides' family homes for the big celebrations.

Twenty-two-year-old Liz Lantz was a little reluctant to attend weddings this season since she had no beau to pair up with during the afternoon festivities. Her bustling tourist business, Amish Buggy Rides, was a needed distraction this time of year. The steady flow of folks who reserved tickets for her Tuesday, Wednesday, and Saturday tours meant she had to dedicate the off days to her household chores. Even so, she was looking forward to the return of her very popular Christmas House Buggy Tour starting the Saturday after Thanksgiving.

Liz still marveled at the number of Englisher folks eager to experience the novelty of a ride in an Amish buggy. That appeal, and Liz's commentary about the sights of her community, which sometimes turned into a bit of storytelling, had quickly given her great word of mouth, bringing new customers beyond the big-city tour buses and her own website. Thankfully, her Mennonite cousin, Roy Miller, had been willing to create and maintain the online site where people could purchase tickets. *A wunnerbaar-gut business*, she thought, grateful each Monday when Roy stopped by with a list of names and tour reservations for the week.

"Coming to Lancaster for a breather has turned out to be one of my better ideas," a smiling middle-aged gentleman with a New Jersey accent had told her just that morning before the first ride of the day. He waited in the partially enclosed wood structure built for her customers adjacent to Hickory Hollow's hardware store.

"If you're looking to relax, you've picked the perfect way," Liz agreed with the congenial man. "We Amish try to take one day at a time, 'specially durin' the busy wedding season."

The man bobbed his head as he stepped closer to hand his

ticket to Liz's nineteen-year-old brother, Adam, her assistant since starting the business two years ago.

Ah, wedding season, thought Liz, who would not be one of the Hickory Hollow brides after all. Her former beau, Calvin Kinsinger, and she had mutually parted ways almost a year ago now, when he moved from the area. And all for the better, it turned out. While Calvin was a pleasant young man, she hadn't missed him as much as she'd expected. Even though she was about the age when most Amish young women were engaged or getting married, Liz knew it was wise to be patient for the right person to come along, someone who wanted similar things in life and entrusted the future to God, for certain.

Thankful for the brisk business on this chilly yet sunny day, Liz welcomed her second group of morning customers, a family of four and a young couple, all wearing puffer jackets and some wrapped in plaid scarves. They boarded the extra-long and extra-wide buggy her father had generously paid to have custom built when she first started offering rides. It had many windows and more space than the traditional family buggy.

Her brother made small talk with the six passengers as they got settled into the enclosed carriage with its handy dashboard heater. While she'd initially protested to her father that it wasn't necessary for her to have Adam go along on these rides—something *Dat* had insisted on to keep her safe when interacting with strangers—she'd come to appreciate what her sometimes reticent brother brought to every excursion with his even-keeled approach and occasional humorous remarks. He had told her, however, that he did not view this part-time job as something that would be permanent, wanting to settle into a full-time job elsewhere and eventually marry.

"*Willkumm*, everyone!" Liz said as Adam stepped away to untie their black Belgian draft horse, King, from the hitching post. "Thanks for joining us for our Amish Back Roads and Tasty Treats Tour."

"Be sure to keep your arms inside the carriage at all times," Adam said as he slid into the front seat and picked up the driving lines. "As we go, my sister Liz here will share some things 'bout Amish life which, honestly, ya might not hear anywhere else." He chuckled.

"Prob'ly so." Liz smiled. "Just leave your cares behind as we ride through beautiful Amish farmland. Today you'll see working windmills, our historic general store, a harness shop, and the one-room schoolhouse Amish children attend until eighth grade. If you have questions along the way, please don't be shy 'bout asking."

Wasting no time, a petite girl sitting with her parents raised her hand. "Does your school have a kindergarten?" she asked.

"Scholars actually start in first grade," Adam replied, "so no kindergarten."

Glancing in the large rearview mirror, Liz noticed the little girl looking up at her mother with big, inquisitive eyes. She paused in case the child had another question, then continued. "Toward the end of the tour, we'll be makin' a stop at our *Aendi* Hannah's for some melt-in-your-mouth cookies and sticky buns. She'll bring the goodies out to the carriage, so for your safety, please stay put when we stop."

Back when Liz was only toying with the notion of possibly starting a buggy-tour enterprise, Aunt Hannah had suggested offering baked goods as part of the ride package. Liz had jumped on the idea, knowing it would provide extra income for their widowed aunt, a baker extraordinaire. Not surprisingly, Adam had declared the baked goods the best part of the tour.

"Now, if everyone is ready and there are no further questions, we'll be on our way." Adam clicked his tongue and directed King past the waiting area, where he and Liz planned to hang a large Christmas wreath with a big red bow in a couple of weeks. Englishers enjoyed the sights and sounds of the holidays, as evidenced by the popularity of last year's Christmas House Buggy Tour. To Liz's delight, many of the bookings were already sold out.

Adam directed the horse with a gentle tug on the left rein, and they headed out of the lot adjacent to the local Amish hardware store owned by *Mamm*'s older brother, *Onkel* Joe, who'd graciously given Liz and Adam permission to meet passengers there. As always when they started out, Liz prayed silently for God's protection over each person in the carriage, thankful for this chance to give customers a laid-back yet enjoyable experience—a little taste of Plain life.

As for Adam, *his* mind was likely focused on Aunt Hannah's tasty treats. Liz smiled at the thought.

While helping make supper that evening, Liz heard Dat talking to Adam at the kitchen table. Not in hushed tones, either, so their conversation wasn't private.

"I need ya to go with me to help build a large addition to my cousin's farmhouse over in Somerset," Dat was saying. "It's a big job. The whole east side of the house will be enlarged—the front room and kitchen—to accommodate their growing family. He and his wife are hoping to have it done in time for Christmas. We'll leave a week from today, bright an' early. They should have all the supplies by then."

"I don't mind, but who'll go with Liz on her buggy rides?" Adam asked, pouring coffee for Dat and himself.

"Oh, I've seen to that already." Dat ran a callused hand through his blond bangs.

Surprised that her father still thought it necessary for her to have someone along on tours, Liz stepped away from the gas range as her plump, blue-eyed *Mamma* came upstairs carrying a quart jar of chow chow. Going over to the table, Liz said, "I couldn't help hearin' what ya said, Dat. How long will yous be gone?"

"Depends on how everything goes, but we should be back by Christmas."

"May I ask who ya lined up to take Adam's place?"

"Matthew Yoder from Bird-in-Hand has agreed to fill in for the time bein'. He's the son of an old friend of mine," Dat explained. "Now that the harvest is in, Matt's been doin' odd jobs and house repairs. But he's glad to pick up a part-time job here and there. Dependable as a pillar, he is."

"So, he'll start next Tuesday, then?" Liz wished she could put an end to the plan. To her thinking, Dat seemed a little too eager for this guy to help out. She didn't know Matt, and she felt anxious about working with a stranger.

Dat nodded. "Matt's a mighty careful driver. I've known him since he cut his first tooth." Her father's lips parted in a half smile. "And he's not spoken for, either."

Liz cringed inwardly—she'd never heard her father say such a thing. Was he that concerned she was still single?

Even Adam's eyebrows rose at this, though Mamm remained silent by the stove.

Martha Rose, Liz's twenty-year-old sister, just coming in from the hen house with a basket of fresh eggs, stood with eyes wide in the doorway of the utility room. She stared at Liz curiously, evidently trying to grasp what Dat had said.

Dat himself filled the awkward silence. "Years ago, I dug a

well with Matt's father and uncle, before Matt was even born. Hardworkin' family they are—with nine fine *Kinner*, too. They're all just as devout as deacons." He nodded approvingly. "And to keep things simple, I've arranged for Matt to come by Amish taxi. He'll meet ya over at the hardware store and return home the same way. I've already paid the fare through just before Christmas."

Adam gave Liz a sympathetic look, but it was apparent there would be no backing down on Dat's part. He'd decided who would fill Adam's place and, stranger or no, that was that.

"Trust me, Lizzy. This'll all work out chust fine." Her father seemed confident enough, but Liz certainly didn't feel the same.

2

Liz's mind was going a mile a minute as she considered the news Dat had given her last evening. Adam seemed to be taking the sudden change of plans in stride, however, as King pulled the tour carriage at an unhurried trot this morning.

When she'd asked him earlier if he was acquainted at all with Matt Yoder, Adam had admitted he was not. "But I wouldn't fret about it, Lizzy. Dat wouldn't've picked him to fill in if he had any concerns."

Liz figured that, but she also knew she would miss the comfortable back-and-forth she and Adam shared during the tours. With her brother, she really only had to think about the customers—something she'd been hard-pressed to do this morning, and he wasn't even gone yet. How would it be with a new guy at her side?

But there was no time to ponder that now. Liz turned toward the passengers seated behind her and put on a smile as she shared a bit of the history of Hickory Hollow. "Back in the 1730s, this plentiful land drew Amish settlers to farm here. My ancestors considered farming a sacred duty. In fact, we still think of plowing and planting the soil as God-given responsibilities—one of the reasons there are so many Amish farmers. My grandfather *Dawdi* Lantz has always said farmin' is the best kind of work."

Adam took over then to talk about the various types of farms found in the community, and it wasn't long before Ella Mae Zook's *Dawdi Haus* came into view. Liz could just imagine the dear woman either brewing peppermint tea or sitting across the table in her home from a friend in need as they sipped tea together. That was her calling, she'd often said—listening to folks as they opened their hearts for her guidance or prayer, or both.

Adam slowed King's trot, and Liz resumed her commentary. "Accordin' to the local grapevine, the delightful woman who lives in that addition might be over one hundred years old, but no one knows for sure. Folks wonder if her family is sworn to secrecy, since none of them has fessed up to the actual number. And whenever the woman is asked, she simply beams and says that one's age really ain't as important as showin' kindness to one's neighbor and followin' the Good Book. Oh, and drinkin' at least one cup of peppermint tea with honey daily."

There was a round of laughter, and even Adam grinned despite having heard this many times before.

A young teen on board raised her hand. "Does her family live in the larger attached house, then?"

"*Jah*, and a short hallway connects her home to her daughter's family, so she has the freedom to live in her own space. But if she needs help or wants to go next door for a meal or a visit, it's convenient."

"We call her the Wise Woman," Adam added, "partly because of her longevity and life experiences, and partly because she gives godly advice when asked for it."

"Sounds like you might know firsthand," an older passenger observed.

"*Puh!* Did I just tell on myself?" Adam chuckled, and a couple of the adults on board muffled a laugh.

Curious, Liz glanced at her brother. She'd never known he'd visited Ella Mae. *Why would he?*

Aunt Hannah's house appeared at the bend of the road, their final stop of this particular tour. Adam made the turn into the driveway and halted the horse. There, waiting on the back stoop, stood Hannah, a short black coat over her long green dress and matching apron, a smile on her rosy cheeks. Her white *Kapp* concealed her graying bun, and her brown eyes shone with welcome as she stepped down into the sunlight and approached the carriage with a rectangular tray of treats.

Liz got out of the carriage to tie King to the hitching post while Adam remained in the driver's seat on the right, where he preferred to be even though he and Liz took turns driving every other tour. *Interacting with customers is my favorite*, she thought as she headed over to meet Aendi Hannah.

To the customers' obvious pleasure, they were given a choice of warm chocolate chip cookies or pumpkin cinnamon rolls with caramel frosting, today's fresh-baked offerings.

Observing her Aendi, Liz thought again of how good it was of her to continue to offer these treats—Liz had had to convince her to do so for a charge, she was that generous. *Her husband, Ammon, was generous, too . . . always directing barn-raisings and never taking a penny for it.* Liz fondly recalled the expert carpenter who had passed away some time ago.

She knew of many others in the hollow who quietly spread kindness without seeking attention for it. Her own Mamm would happily drop everything to help stitch up a wedding or anniversary quilt or to make knotted comforters to donate to Christian

Aid Ministries for the poor around the world. Liz respected such big-heartedness and tried to reflect that in her own life, too.

After the final tour of the day, she and Adam rode home past Logan Hyatt's big spread of land, one of very few farms owned by Englishers in the heart of the hollow. Logan and his wife, Ashley, had managed to outbid the Amish bishop about fifteen months ago, getting things off on the wrong foot with not just Bishop John Beiler but his newly married nephew, who'd hoped to rent the home from his uncle. Like other Plain communities, the Hickory Hollow Amish preferred to keep farmland in the family and out of the hands of the English, especially with a farm like this that had been Amish-owned for generations.

Much like their neighbors, Logan and his family kept to themselves, but immediately after moving in, they did something that put them at odds with everyone around them: They installed electricity in the house and the barn, and even put in outdoor sensor lighting.

Then, last November, the Hyatts began to lavishly decorate for Christmas. It was nothing short of shocking, considering that, except for Ella Mae's simple wreath, not a single house around the hollow was decorated, and certainly not with outdoor lights.

When, in addition to a spotlighted nativity scene with its own angel chorus, there appeared a multitude of decorated trees, a gaggle of dancing elves in the side yard, and a large Santa with a sleigh and reindeer on the roof, the People's eyebrows rose all the higher. Some folks got quite *ferhoodled*, wondering what might next appear.

On the day after Thanksgiving, when the display lit up for the first time, the complaining began in earnest. Some even said the neighboring Amish children were having trouble sleeping, and barn animals were becoming distressed—Liz had heard several wild spins on the matter. In her own family, the Hyatts' property had been a subject for discussion around the kitchen table as they decided whether to ignore the massive light display or try to accept it since, as Dat pointed out, they had little hope of influencing their Englisher neighbors to take it down.

Then things became more tense when the English heard about the Christmas House in the midst of Amish farmland and began coming in droves, clogging up the narrow roads, some cars even sliding into snowy ditches, making it unsafe for horse-drawn buggies to pass through the area. And all for a look-see at Logan Hyatt's over-the-top display. Amish up and down the hollow talked about how senseless it was to spend so much money on decorations and electricity, let alone bring bedlam to the formerly peaceful farm community, disrupting their way of life. Because of the extra traffic, some Amish dairy farmers had a terrible time getting home for the late-afternoon milking, after running errands in town.

Others, primarily Englishers, had a different spin, saying that the Christmas House spread happiness and cheer, building anticipation for the big day. While Liz was aware of the conflicting opinions about the extravaganza and its accompanying loud music, the tourists who took her buggy rides were obvious fans, and the flashy house brought in good business for her. Torn between the People's opinions and knowing how much her customers loved seeing the Christmas House from a horse-drawn buggy, Liz decided not to take a stance.

"Why do ya think the Hyatts picked Hickory Hollow to live and farm?" Adam questioned as they headed toward home.

Liz had wondered about this, too. "It's a mystery, for sure."

Once home, Liz headed upstairs to her room and sat on her bed. She spotted an unfinished navy-blue knit scarf on the chair near the window. That, along with the already completed matching knit hat, was a potential Christmas gift for someone, although she didn't know who just yet. Last year, she'd made two sets like this, one for Dat and the other for Adam. But for some reason, she had started this one. *Was I hoping to meet someone?*

Reclining now, she shrugged the thought away, thankful that at least Martha Rose had a beau. Liz's younger sister was such a good help to Mamm and to Dat, looking after the chickens and gathering eggs in the hen house, selling the excess to the neighbors.

Presently, Liz heard footsteps in the hallway and opened her eyes to see her fair-haired sister holding a letter, undoubtedly from Ben Fisher, Daniel Fisher's nephew. Ben had been dating Martha for quite a while now.

Liz smiled. "From your beau?"

"He's getting more serious here lately," Martha replied, a few strands of hair coming out from beneath her blue bandana. She sat down on the edge of the bed, suddenly looking solemn. "The thing is," Martha said more quietly, "I feel bad that *you* aren't seein' anyone, Lizzy."

"Oh, I've been fine since Calvin and I split up. Really." She sat up and reached for her sister's hand. "Don't worry 'bout me."

"You're sure?"

Liz nodded. "I want nothin' more than for you to enjoy your courtship with Ben, sister."

A faint smile appeared, and Martha gave her hand a squeeze before leaving the room to read her letter, causing Liz to wonder if Martha also felt hesitant about seriously courting since she was the younger sister.

3

That Sunday, Liz and Martha Rose rode with Adam to Singing at sundown in his black open buggy. It was a tight squeeze, but thankfully the preacher's farmhouse was only a short jaunt away. Even so, Liz had to sit sideways to fit in the slim space between the edge of the courting carriage and her slender sister.

There was no moon in sight, but the tawny glow of gas lamps in neighbors' kitchen windows cast light on the surrounding furrowed fields. Liz could scarcely wait for the first snowfall, when Dat would let her use his large sleigh with its built-in seating for her tours. The horse-drawn sleigh made rides all the more festive and fun, especially for folks on the Christmas House Buggy Tour, who always enjoyed the finale of traveling past the show of lights, life-sized nativity scene, Santa and reindeer, holiday music, and everything else related to Christmas. Without snow on the ground, though, her custom-made carriage and the merry bells hanging from King's harness would have to suffice.

Adam broke the stillness. "Will you be all right on your own after Singin', Martha?"

"I believe so."

"So happy for ya, sister," Liz whispered.

"If need be, I can drop ya off at home, Liz," Adam offered.

"If ya don't mind, I'd appreciate it," Liz said, a little disappointed at the prospect of having to ride home with her sibling yet again.

Stars sparkled as they appeared, and Liz wondered if she'd ever dare ask Adam about his visit to Ella Mae's, recalling what he'd said the other day about her godly advice. She smiled in the fading light, squished next to Martha Rose though she was. Maybe there'd never be a good time, and besides, it wasn't her place to question his doings. Nevertheless, she had a hard time imagining her younger brother seeking counsel . . . or drinking tea of any kind, for that matter.

Adam pulled into the preacher's driveway and jumped out to tie King to the post across the driveway from the back porch. Entering the house, Liz and Martha headed downstairs, where the Singing was to take place. For now, they sat with the other girls sixteen and older. With their two older sisters married and busy with two small children each, Liz and Martha were each other's best companion. And Liz was grateful, especially after the breakup last year. *Martha made sure I was not alone at youth gatherings.*

Soon, two of their girl cousins joined them, and Liz and Martha moved over to make room. Liz greeted Fran and Naomi warmly, Fran being almost as close as another sister, though more so to Martha Rose.

Just now, Liz noticed Martha stealing glances across the table in Ben Fisher's direction. *How serious are they?* Liz wondered. *If I were already wed, would they be getting married this wedding season? Ach, do they think they must wait another year because of me?*

Liz glanced discreetly at the young men around the room and realized that, once again, there were no new faces amongst them.

Inwardly, she sighed and wondered if it made sense for her to keep attending the gatherings when no one there was likely to ask her riding—most of the eligible young men in attendance had already paired up with someone, and none of the others sparked her interest, really.

Am I too picky?

As she waited there on the bench for the Singing to begin, Liz thought back to a discussion she'd had with Dat more than two years ago, before she'd started her business. . . .

Liz and her father leaned on the white fence on the perimeter of the barnyard, observing the grazing mules in the near distance. The July morning was hot and sultry, and the meadow was profuse with golden dandelions, some already gone to seed.

Liz contemplated how to begin. "Dat," she said, forging ahead at last, "there's somethin' I'd like to discuss with ya." Slowly, she began to share her desire to offer buggy rides to tourists. "Not as a livelihood, though. I want to work only three days a week, but with what I'd be chargin', I could still give ya a nice amount for room and board."

Turning to study her, Dat was silent at first. "No need to work outside the home, Lizzy." He glanced at the bluing sky, clouds skittering off toward the east.

"It's somethin' I'd *like* to do, though."

Her father removed his straw hat and fanned his perspiring brow. "Workin' in a job like that means you'd be rubbin' shoulders with outsiders." He reminded her that spending time with worldly folk—in a confined space, no less—wasn't the wisest choice for a single, young Amish woman.

She'd prepared herself for this. "Well, I'm a baptized church member an' committed to God, Dat. Don't worry that I'd stray."

"Still, there's temptation on every side."

Liz couldn't deny that. "But what if it was a way to let my light shine to folks I might never meet otherwise, and maybe even to glorify God, too?" She quoted Matthew five, verse sixteen, one of her favorites since childhood. "'Let your light so shine before men, that they may see your good works, and glorify your Father which is in heaven.'"

Dat bobbed his head slowly. "Do ya really think takin' Englishers on rides would accomplish that?"

"Why not?"

He paused yet again. "Well then, here's somethin' else to think on: What if you married after ya got started with these tours? Your husband might not want ya workin' amongst the world or at all, 'specially not once you start a family. Have ya considered that?"

"Well, plenty of Hickory Hollow married women work away from home at quilt shops and as waitresses," she pointed out. "But I agree that a family must come first. Right now, though, that might not be a concern for me."

She contemplated what to say next. "Honestly, though, it'd be interesting to talk to new people and maybe even quash some Amish myths floating around."

Although running a buggy tour business was a little unusual for a single Amishwoman, her father had ultimately given his permission, but only on the condition that Adam accompany her, an arrangement she'd quickly come to appreciate. Her father was a sensible and caring man, after all.

Sitting up straighter now, Liz was glad to see Preacher Yoder and his wife coming downstairs to give their welcome. After several announcements, including one about an upcoming hayride and barbeque, everyone sang the birthday song for those with November celebrations.

Then Preacher Yoder's wife blew into her pitch pipe and started the first gospel song of the evening, "I'll Meet You in the Morning." As was customary, they sang the verses in German and the chorus in English, switching easily between the two languages.

Liz joined her voice with those of the other *Youngie*, glad to make a joyful noise unto the Lord. *I need to focus on what matters.*

Whatever tonight and the coming days might bring, she would continue to pray for the right fellow to come along, someone who shared her hope to bring encouragement, even blessings, to others.

4

Liz's father and Adam departed for Somerset before dawn that Tuesday, leaving Liz to confide her concerns to Mamm about having a stranger ride with her today. "I know Dat wants to help, but I'm not so sure I actually need anyone to step in," she said as she warmed up the leftover cornmeal mush while Mamm fried some eggs. "Do you know anything 'bout this guy?"

"Only what your father said. He's spoken of the family several times to me over the years." Mamm turned off the gas flame and set the eggs aside to await Martha Rose's return from feeding the chickens.

"Did Dat ask Martha 'bout this?"

"Are ya wonderin' why he didn't ask her to go with ya?" Mamm asked.

"Honestly, I hadn't thought of that, but now that ya brought it up . . ."

"*Nee.*" Mamm shook her head. "Things are set in place. No need to fret, Lizzy. Besides, your Dat wants ya safe on the roads come December. Remember how last year he got sideswiped by a car comin' from the Christmas House? It's a blessing he escaped in one piece. Having an extra set of eyes in the front of the touring carriage is right *schmaert* with customers to tend to, too."

Liz had never forgotten how shaken Mamm was that day, and how distressed her dear father had been. *Dat's right*, she thought more agreeably, and decided that she must make the best of working with Matt Yoder.

Who knows, he might just be a nice fellow.

At eight-thirty that morning, Liz was met near the waiting area at Onkel Joe's hardware store by a tall young Amishman with light brown hair. Apart from his straw hat, he was dressed in church clothes, all in black except his white shirt, and he carried a black horse-grooming tote along with an insulated lunch bag.

He walked right over to her. "I'm Matthew Yoder," he said, shaking her hand. "But please call me Matt. *Gut* to meet ya. You must be Liz."

She nodded, taking note of his self-assurance. "You're right on time."

"I want to make sure we start things off on the right foot," he said, hazel eyes twinkling.

She was about to ask if her father had explained what Adam did to assist her on the buggy rides when, at that moment, her Onkel Joe stepped out of the hardware store, walking this way. "Lizzy, can I have a word?"

She excused herself from Matt and went to meet her uncle. "Everything all right?"

"So, your Dat and *Bruder* are off to Somerset."

She nodded. "They're building a large addition onto a house there. One of your mutual cousins. Sounds like a big job."

"Your Dat filled me in. And made a point of sayin' he doesn't want your Mamm, or you and Martha Rose, havin' to do the men's work in the barn."

Liz recalled hearing Dat tell Mamm this very thing before he and Adam left town.

"So while they're gone, I'll be lookin' after yous."

"My two married brothers are pitchin' in, too," Liz told him.

"*Des gut.* Not much to do this time of year, but the barn will be kept clean and mucked out . . . bedding straw freshened, and livestock fed and watered." Onkel Joe paused. "And if there's anything else ya need, let me know. We're just up the road."

"*Denki*, Onkel."

He nodded, his gaze drifting inquisitively toward Matthew. "Looks like ya got yourself a new sidekick."

"Just 'til Adam's back."

Onkel Joe frowned and shook his head. "He sure looks familiar."

"His name's Matthew Yoder. Maybe ya know his father? Dat does. The family lives in Bird-in-Hand."

Her uncle shrugged. "Not sure where I would've met him."

Liz didn't know Matt well enough to invite Onkel Joe over to talk with him. Besides, the ticket holders for the first tour would be arriving any minute.

"I'll noodle on it," Onkel Joe said. "Have yourself a nice day." He pushed his thick fingers through his shaggy brown beard, glancing again at Matt.

Liz hurried back to the horse and carriage where Matt stood. She quickly filled him in on the family of five who'd scheduled a private tour for the wife's birthday. "By the way, I'll do the drivin' today," she said, wanting to get that settled. "That'll give you an idea of the route and the pace." Thankfully, Matt only nodded. "On this tour, we'll ride past a few dairy farms, then over to my

Dat's brother's place to see their greenhouse and a quilt shop. Then a little something fun for the children, and last of all, a birthday surprise."

Matt grinned. "Sounds like a green thumb and someone with an eye for colorful quilts might be on board."

Liz couldn't help smiling at his observations. "Exactly."

"So ya give custom-made tours, then?" Matt asked, looking somewhat out of place in his for-good clothing. Dat must not have told him to wear everyday clothes. *Or maybe*, she thought, slightly embarrassed, *he wanted Matt to make a good impression on me.*

"*Jah*, private tours for any occasion, as well as the set tours popular this time of year." She mentioned the Amish Back Roads and Tasty Treats Tour, and the Amish Farm Tour. "Oh, and real soon, the Christmas House Buggy Tour."

Matt tilted his head and frowned. "Christmas House, ya say?"

"Just a little over a mile away."

"I helped paint some rooms and install some shelving there last year when I was working part-time for a local contractor. Got to know the new owner a little, Logan Hyatt. He told me he liked to decorate for the season to make up for the years he missed out on celebrating Christmas as a child."

"Ya mean his family didn't celebrate?"

"From what he said, his father was opposed to it."

"I wonder why."

"Well, Logan never volunteered why, but when he got married, he said he'd promised his wife they would celebrate Christmas merrily and in a big way, and not only in their hearts."

This interested Liz. "So *that's* the reason for all the outdoor decorations."

"And indoors, too," Matt said. "A tree in nearly every room. I've never seen a family go all out for a holiday like that."

"That's somethin'. No Amish would go to such lengths."

"He and his wife are new to Lancaster County. They were real kind to me those few days I worked on the house . . . seemed eager for company. That's when Logan showed me all the Christmas trees—real ones, fake ones, cloth ones, you name it."

"Did he ever say why they moved here?" she asked, still very curious.

"Never did, and I didn't ask."

A minivan turned into the parking lot just then, and a man, woman, and three children got out, all of them smiling.

"*Willkuum!* Such a nice sunny day for your birthday buggy ride," Liz said, smiling at the woman. "I think you'll enjoy it."

Cody Nolt cheerfully introduced himself, his wife, Patricia, and their three children, all of them homeschooled—nine-year-old Danica and six-year-old identical twins, Jack and James. "We've all been looking forward to this," Cody told her. "When I ran across your website, I knew this was the perfect present for Patricia." He glanced affectionately at his wife.

"I'm so glad," Liz replied, once again grateful for her Mennonite cousin's help in setting up and maintaining the site that handled her reservations and ticket sales. She doubted her business would be this steady without Roy's help. Liz looked at each of the sweet-faced children. "I've planned a special tour *and* a surprise for your mamma."

Then she introduced Matt Yoder as her assistant, and he greeted the family cordially and accepted their tickets.

Soon, they were on their way and passing the general store when one of the look-alike twins spoke up. "We saw the Christmas House Tour online. Does that tour come with cake, too . . . like today's?"

And with that, the birthday cake secret was out! Glancing in the rearview mirror, Liz saw Cody and his daughter, Danica, both shaking their heads.

Liz ignored the spilled beans and instead answered the question about goodies. "There'll be plenty-a sweets for that Christmas tour, *jah*, but you'll have to come an' see for yourself," she teased.

"Okay!" the boy shouted, grinning at his twin.

Cody chuckled and slipped his arm around his wife.

"Today we'll be goin' to an Amish petting farm that belongs to my father's youngest brother and his wife," Liz told them. "Years ago, after marrying and wantin' to start their family, Onkel Caleb and Aendi Elsie adopted two little orphaned sisters. Once the girls were settled into their new home and enjoyed helping round the farm, they asked to adopt a pair of goats."

The twins on board giggled.

"So my uncle and aunt decided they would purchase two goats. But do ya think that was enough?"

The children shook their heads.

"That's right. Perty soon the girls wanted even more animals to care for."

"Did they ask for two puppies, maybe?" Danica asked softly.

"*Jah*, and two miniature horses, too," Liz said, holding the driving lines steady as a car passed by. "Not long after that, they added two donkeys . . . and then two llamas."

"Like Noah and the ark!" the twins said gleefully in unison.

Now the whole family was laughing.

"Wow, what animals *don't* they have?" young James asked.

"You'll find out real soon," Matt replied, speaking for the first time since the ride began. "Remember, it's a farm with a petting zoo. You'll be able to get up close to everything."

"Yay!" the twins cheered.

Liz slowed the horse as they came upon two dairy farms, the boys' noses pressed against the windows as they pointed to the grazing cattle. Their more reserved sister also watched with curiosity but remained silent.

Later, during the short tour of the greenhouse, Liz took notice of Matt, who leaned over to talk and laugh with little Jack and James like a good friend or relative might. *He must have younger siblings or nephews and nieces.*

As an extra bonus, Liz's Onkel Caleb swung them by the barn and took all of them up to the hayloft, showing where hay was stored for the winter. "This is also where we host the Singing gatherings for the Amish youth every other Sunday evening during the spring, summer, and fall when it's our turn," he explained.

Cody pulled out his phone to take a photo of his children sitting atop a large square bale. First a silly pose, then a smiley one.

The time spent in the quilt shop was largely for Patricia's benefit, but Matt entertained the children near the checkout counter, taking a quarter out of his pocket and spinning it. Soon, all of them were taking turns to see who could keep the coin spinning the longest while Matt counted the seconds.

Meanwhile, Liz enjoyed Elsie's descriptions of the Amish quilt patterns on display. After listening intently, Patricia chose a quilt she "had to have," a lovely Double Nine Patch in shades of green and yellow and brown. "A special birthday gift for myself," she told Liz, eyes bright.

Once the queen-size quilt was wrapped and paid for, Elsie invited everyone around to the large fenced-in area where the animals were located. A quarter in the food-dispenser slot produced a handful of feed, more than either Jack or James could manage to hold with their hands cupped together. Matt, anticipating the possibility of spillage, quickly held his hands beneath theirs.

Cody took photos of the llamas while his wife tutted to one of the small donkeys who'd nosed through the nearby fence.

Soon, she was petting the donkey's head as the miniature horses made a beeline across the barnyard, two sheep close behind, making their way toward Jack and James and their generous handfuls of feed.

Arms folded, Danica wandered over to Liz, observing. "The llamas are so tall," she said with a grimace. "And they spit."

"They are tall, but they spit at each other and scarcely ever at people, unless they're aggravated." Liz looked at Danica; the sun shone on the girl's shoulder-length blond hair. "When I was your age, I wasn't fond of them, either. But now, chickens . . . I loved *them*."

Danica's blue eyes lit up. "You raised chickens?"

"My family still does." Liz went on to say that her younger sister and she had been warned by their father when they were little never to treat them as pets or to name them. "But it was so hard not to."

"Why couldn't you name them?" Danica asked, a puzzled look on her round face.

"Can ya guess why not?" Liz disliked revealing this part.

Danica's face crumpled like she was trying to figure it out. Then the light seemed to dawn. "Oh yeah, because someday they'd be your dinner."

"That's right."

Frowning, Danica said, "I don't blame you for wanting to give them names, though."

Liz smiled. How she hoped the Good Lord would someday bless her with inquisitive children like Danica and her younger brothers.

First, though, a husband, she thought. *Well, first a beau . . . then a husband, Lord willing.*

Onkel Caleb invited all of them into the large farmhouse, where Elsie had already laid out a pretty yellow tablecloth with sunflower dessert plates. A three-layer chocolate cake with chocolate frosting looked enticing there in the center of the trestle table.

"Sit wherever yous like," Elsie told them, her dimpled cheeks pink.

Once they were seated, Onkel Caleb bowed his head for a silent prayer, and everyone else did, too.

Afterward, Liz was surprised when Matt quietly led out in singing the birthday song for Patricia, and everyone else joined in. Again, Liz was conscious of Matt's exceptional manners and comfortable way around people, anticipating their needs.

So far, he's actually working out okay.

5

A brief downpour did not keep folks from traveling to the two Amish weddings a short distance apart. The many gray buggies parked at the brides' parents' homes left the roads all but vacant by nine o'clock.

Since Liz didn't offer buggy rides on Thursdays, she was available to run errands this morning for Mamm, and today Martha Rose had asked to ride along, once her usual egg customers had stopped by. The sky was clearing now, the kind of November day that gave hope that winter might be milder this year or, wishful thinking, not come at all.

Liz took their older horse, Charlie, to the general store, where she and Martha shopped for a few items Mamm had requested, as well as coconut oil and corn syrup to make a big batch of peppermint taffy. The colorful taffy was one of the many goodies their mother liked to have on hand for the grandchildren at Christmas, though everyone loved Mamm's special recipe. Even though it would have been easier to just purchase taffy tomorrow at the Friday market in Bird-in-Hand, they kept on with the tradition of making it from scratch, not wanting to miss out on the fun of pulling taffy at home, their hands all slathered with butter.

After the grocery items were stored in the back of the buggy, Liz and Martha headed over to their deacon's house to drop off three knotted comforters Mamm had made to donate to the Christian Aid Ministries. The deacon would then hire a van driver to take the comforters and other donations to Ephrata, where they would later be shipped to the clothing center in Shipshewana, Indiana.

As they rode, Liz offered a silent prayer for each recipient who would be made warm because of Mamm's generosity. Once the donations were dropped off, Liz and Martha returned to the horse and carriage, the weather still unseasonably pleasant for November.

"Anything else you'd like to do?" Liz asked her sister as they opened the buggy doors and climbed in.

"Could we drop by Ella Mae's to say hullo, and then go to the library?" Martha closed the carriage door on her side. "I need somethin' new to read."

Liz agreed. "Wouldn't think of denying the bookworm in our house." She grinned as she reached for the driving lines.

"Well, you could read more, too, but you take people on buggy rides instead," Martha replied, smiling at her. "Ya don't exactly have much leisure time, do ya?"

"I like to keep busy, ya know."

They rode a ways in silence, Martha looking out the windshield on her side until she turned to Liz, breaking the quiet. "I forgot to ask how things went with the new guy along on your buggy rides the last two days."

"Better than expected."

"That's *gut*." Martha folded her arms. "I'm perty sure Dat wanted to pair ya up with him while Adam's in Somerset.

Maybe just an excuse to do a little matchmakin'." She gave a little chuckle. "Who knew Dat had it in him?"

Liz recalled what Dat had said about Matt not being spoken for. "You won't believe it, but Matt groomed King after every two tours—once after the mornin' ones and then again midafternoon."

"Goodness."

Liz nodded. "I told him that Adam only did that first thing in the mornin' and then at the end of the day after we returned home. Between tours, there's really not a lot of time for horse grooming."

Martha was quiet for a moment. "Maybe Matt's tryin' to go the extra mile so he can keep workin' with ya even after Adam returns."

"Oh, he can make more money being a handyman. Besides, the understanding with Dat was that he's just fillin' in during Adam's absence."

"Hmm," Martha murmured, then gave her a teasing grin. "If ya say so."

Liz glanced at her sister, wondering why she seemed so certain about the motivations of a young man she'd never met.

Ella Mae greeted them at the back door with her usual sweet smile on her deeply lined face and invited them inside. "I have some fresh tea a-brewin'." There was that familiar sparkle in her big blue eyes, like she was expecting them. Liz found this very appealing, even curious. No matter when she'd come to visit, Ella Mae always made her feel welcomed.

Liz and Martha took their places on one side of the small square table near the kitchen window. The sunlight poured in, warming them, and the house filled with the lovely scent of honey-sweetened peppermint tea.

"It's your day off, Liz, ain't so?" Ella Mae said, bringing a floral teapot over and setting it down.

Liz smiled at this. "You remembered."

"Ain't much I miss, dearie."

Martha exchanged a glance with her sister. "Let me help ya with the cups and saucers." She scooted her chair back.

Liz doubted Ella Mae would comply, but she did, going over to the cupboard with Martha.

"See the matching floral ones up there?" Ella Mae pointed to the second shelf of her cupboard.

Martha nodded and took them down carefully.

Once they were seated, Ella Mae prayed aloud as she was known to do for even tea and cookies. She wasn't shy about it and let visiting folks know that it was important to be grateful for the little things, too. When it came to matters of faith and the heart, the elderly woman was always plainspoken, and Liz found it refreshing.

One of a kind!

Ella Mae poured tea into their cups. "I've been thinkin' it's 'bout time for us to talk, Liz, since I s'pose you're doin' those Christmas House Buggy Tours again this year."

"*Jah*," Liz replied, suspecting what was coming. The woman had a heart of gold.

"*Des gut*, then. Bring your riders by again at the end of that late-afternoon tour for hot cocoa and cookies."

Liz paused, wanting to be considerate of Ella Mae's health and time when the woman moved more slowly every year. "I realize it's extra work, so just know I'm not askin'."

Ella Mae chuckled lightly. "Well, I'm offerin'. So don't think too hard on this." Ella Mae's bespectacled eyes met hers over her teacup.

"Well, if ya really want to, it's only right that ya receive somethin' in return . . . like we agreed on last year."

"*Ach*, it's such a joy to see everyone in such a cheery mood an' all, outsiders or not. It's *gut* to celebrate the Lord's birthday with folk."

Liz felt the same way. But she recalled how hard it had been to convince Ella Mae to accept any payment last year. After all, the woman had to bake a new batch of cookies three times a week, and there was the cost of her delicious homemade cocoa mix and extra milk, too. "I'd feel better if ya'd let me at least reimburse ya. It's only fair."

Ella Mae gave a mischievous little shrug. "How 'bout I decide what's fair?"

Martha giggled a little. "*Glotzkopp*—yous both are." Her giggle now turned into an outright laugh, and Ella Mae joined in.

"*Jah*, s'pose there *are* a few of us stubborn folks round here," Liz replied, reaching for the pretty teacup and taking a sip.

At that, Ella Mae's eyes shone, but Liz noticed that she still hadn't agreed to take any compensation.

At the library, Liz sat in the buggy while Martha headed inside. As she waited, Liz unexpectedly found herself wondering what Matt was doing today. He had such a way with people that it was hard to imagine him wanting to do any other type of work, really. So maybe Martha was right, maybe he *was* buttering Liz up by frequently grooming King.

Nee, she thought, *he's just fond of our horse. . . .*

6

After the noon meal that day, Liz washed the dishes and Martha dried them as Mamm gathered the ingredients to make peppermint taffy. Once done, Martha greased a baking sheet, and Liz sprayed the kitchen scissors, a pair of rubber gloves, and a metal spatula with cooking spray. Meanwhile, Mamm stirred the syrup in a medium saucepan, bringing it to a boil. When the syrup had begun cooling, Mamm slipped on the oiled gloves and began to maneuver it back and forth with the help of the metal spatula until Liz and Martha, who'd buttered their hands, could pick it up and begin pulling it, cool enough now to handle.

Twisting and pulling the candy was the most fun for Liz. Since the taffy would harden rather quickly, she and Martha wasted no time creating a long rope, talking and laughing all the while. How Liz enjoyed Martha's company, especially working together in the kitchen. It was a blessing they were only two years apart in age.

While they worked the taffy, Mamm slipped out of the kitchen, heading upstairs to write a letter to Dat.

The wonderful-good aroma of peppermint filled the house,

and Liz breathed it in deeply, relishing it as she always had for as long as she could remember pulling taffy with Martha. "The scent of peppermint reminds me of our childhood," she told Martha. "And of visits to Ella Mae's."

"It's always such fun to see her, but I've never gone for advice," Martha said, then added, "though I'm sure I might need to someday. Seems like everyone round here turns to her at some point." She was suddenly quiet for a moment, like more was on her mind. "Did ya know that even Adam went to see her a year ago?" Martha said, the taffy already starting to get glossy and light-colored. "Mamm mentioned this to me recently, so I don't think it's a secret."

Liz remembered what Adam had said about the Wise Woman last week during a tour.

"He wanted Ella Mae to pray with him 'bout his future." Martha looked solemn just then. "I had asked Mamm how she knew Dat was the right choice of a mate for her, and that's how Adam's visit to Ella Mae came up."

"Ah, no wonder."

Martha nodded. "Adam wanted to seek God's will 'bout whether he should stay in Hickory Hollow or not."

"But he was already baptized, so why would he want to leave?" Liz felt very surprised to learn this. With all the time she and Adam spent working together, she'd never sensed he might not want to make a home for himself here.

"Well," Martha continued, "a perty girl at Lapp's Farm Market had evidently caught his attention, and they'd started going out—remember when he stopped attending Singings with us for a while? Accordin' to Mamm, Adam believed he was falling for her. Of course, he could've easily talked to Dat 'bout it, but I guess he wanted advice from someone impartial like Ella Mae . . . like a lot of folks do, ya know."

"The girl was Amish?" Liz asked as she reached for the scissors coated with cooking spray. She began to cut the soft and chewy candy into small pieces and placed them on the baking sheets to cool, her mouth watering as she did so.

"*Jah*, but she was from a church district in Ronks. She had suggested Adam could work for her father in a welding shop there once they were married."

"*Ach*, really?" Liz couldn't imagine a job less suited to her outdoorsy brother.

"Sounds like she had things all figured out . . . a bit pushy, if ya ask me." Martha shook her head. "Of course if she loved him, she prob'ly would've wanted to join Adam here in the hollow once they wed."

Liz sighed. "Well, there *are* fellas who move to the girl's community, too."

Nodding, Martha said, "Ella Mae must've urged Adam to put the whole thing in God's hands."

Liz agreed. "The Lord cares 'bout every inch of our lives." She thought of her own repeated prayers for a husband, and how she had once hoped Calvin was the right one until it became clear his priorities were very different from hers. *I'd like someone who joins me in shining God's light to others, even in the small ways.*

After the peppermint candy had completely cooled, they each sampled a delicious piece, then wrapped the rest in wax paper, winding the ends to keep the taffies fresh.

Later, following evening Bible reading and prayer with Mamm and Martha, Liz thought again about Adam seeking out Ella Mae Zook. *God must've answered right quick*, she pondered, going upstairs to make additional rows in the knitted navy-blue scarf, something she enjoyed doing to relax at day's end.

7

Saturday morning, Liz groomed King, Dat's gentle giant, before hitching him to the touring carriage and heading over to Onkel Joe's hardware store. She would remind Matt that he didn't have to groom the horse after the second tour this morning.

She arrived earlier than usual at the meeting area and went into the store to the back break room to look over her notebook. Wind gusts had awakened her in the night, making it hard to fall back to sleep, so she poured herself a second cup of coffee.

Onkel Joe appeared in the doorway and sat down with her at the small table. "Say, Lizzy, I've been a-thinkin' 'bout where I ran into your new tour assistant."

"Oh?"

A slow smile spread across his face. "It dawned on me when Logan Hyatt came in recently to purchase some extension cords. S'pose he's gettin' his house ready for another big Christmas show."

Liz noticed her uncle's quick frown.

"Last year, Matt came in here several times, hired by Logan to help do some jobs at the house after he and his family moved in."

"So . . . the mystery's solved."

Joe nodded. "Seems like a responsible young man."

Dat thinks so, too, she mused, nodding.

Glancing at the wall clock, Liz realized it was time to take the last few sips of coffee and get back outside. She left a dollar bill on the table for the coffee.

Liz buttoned her black coat as she walked back out into the brisk morning. She could see Matt Yoder exiting the nine-passenger van—what folks liked to call the Amish taxi—dressed in everyday clothes again, just as he was on Wednesday. Matt waved, his lunch bag and that black grooming tote at his side once again.

When he met her in the covered waiting area, she told him, "Say, I groomed King this mornin' at home . . . didn't want you to have to durin' your lunch break."

"Well, hullo to you, too." Matt grinned as he put the tote in the back of the carriage.

She felt her face heat. "*Ach*, hullo," she said, flustered at having gotten ahead of herself.

Matt smiled. "I don't mind groomin' King, really. He's a beauty."

"But my Dat surely didn't ask ya to, did he?"

Matt chuckled. "I'm just s'posed to do whatever ya need done."

Now Liz had to smile.

"And to make sure you're safe on the narrow roads round here." He beamed back at her.

"Well," Liz said, "I really think that's just when the snowy roads can sometimes be a tight squeeze."

"'Specially with all the folks comin' to see the Christmas House."

She explained that she took her tours past the Hyatts' display well before the nightly parade of cars showed up. "Last year, Ashley Hyatt noticed my tours and began to switch the lights on right around twilight, and it's just beautiful. Not the same as seein' the display when it's totally dark, but it's fine."

"*Des schmaert.* Don't see how a big carriage like this one could manage that crowded road otherwise."

She told Matt about Dat's frightening accident last year, when he'd been knocked nearly off the road—sideswiped by a skidding car. "Fortunately, the driver's insurance covered the cost of repairs to the buggy. But it was a miracle that Dat and our old horse, Charlie, escaped with only bumps and bruises."

"The hand of the Lord."

"That's what Dat said, too."

Matt nodded. "Say, have ya heard from your brother . . . or your Dat?"

"Well, not yet. Mamm'll prob'ly hear soon. They'll exchange letters a couple times a week."

"Just curious if they know yet how long they'll be gone."

"Dat plans to be home for Christmas, but they might be able to get back sooner if things go well."

Going over to the horse, Matt approached from the left side and rubbed King's long, graceful neck and nose. Then he slowly held out his hand flat and offered two sugar cubes. "Well, I hope it's for longer, so we can get better acquainted," he told Liz, smiling.

Her heart did a little flip. *Surely he doesn't mean anything by that. . . .*

Not sure what to say, she asked, "What did ya do yesterday?"

"Oh, besides workin' with my Dat in the barn, I shelved donated canned goods at a food pantry for the poor. They need volunteers, so I'm happy to help."

"*Wunnerbaar.* Have you been doin' this for a while?"

"Oh, a few months, *jah.* I prefer to keep busy, even when there's a lull in my part-time work. So I put in nearly a day's work there whenever I can. It's a practical kind of ministry, which I like."

Matt's comments resonated with her, and she was glad she'd stuck her neck out to ask.

The day was cloudy and cooler than recent days had been, but when her customers showed up, they were excited for every tour. And full of questions.

Surprisingly, today Matt shared a few anecdotes of his own—including what it was like to live without electricity or cars—"what Englishers might call 'living off the grid.'" Liz wondered if he was just naturally wanting to share with the customers, or if he was trying to show her that he could help with commentary, too.

During their lunch break before the two afternoon Amish Farm Tours, Liz encouraged him to "feel free to interject here and there like ya did earlier."

"I should've discussed it with ya first."

She shook her head. "I'll look forward to any interesting things you'd like to add."

"Okay, then," he said. "We're a team."

His face lit up with another of his disarming grins, and she took another bite of her sandwich, trying not to smile too much.

By now the temperature had dropped since the morning tours, and she was glad she'd worn a sweater beneath her short black coat. It was nearly mid-November, and she could almost feel the coming of more wintry weather.

One customer asked if there were additional times for the Christmas House Buggy Tour beyond those listed on the website or the flyer they'd picked up in the Lancaster County tourism bureau.

"*Denki* for askin'. But that particular tour is only at three-thirty on Tuesdays, Wednesdays, and Saturdays, like last year. Due to safety, I don't give rides after dark. I'm sure you understand."

"Have you ever thought of adding more carriages?" another passenger asked, a woman wearing a white cup-shaped prayer *Kapp* who sat with an Englisher man. "If so, I'd be happy to help with drivin'. I was raised Amish, so I have years of experience."

Liz hardly knew how to respond. She'd never personally known anyone in Hickory Hollow who'd left the Amish and had only heard of one—Katie Lapp Fisher—but that was decades ago. "I'll have to think on that," she said, hoping to dismiss the question.

"Might we talk after the tour?" the woman pressed, glancing at her guy friend.

"Sure," Liz agreed, wondering what more the woman might have to say.

She returned to her planned narration and shared about the upcoming dairy farm, where they'd be riding along the field lanes and eventually seeing the inside of the two-story barn. "We won't see the actual milking, since that takes place early morning and late afternoon."

Later, after that tour was finished and she was alone with the Plain woman while Matt tended to King, Liz explained to her that working at home and around her parents' farm was her first priority. "I really don't have any plans to expand my business, at least for now. The rides are just a hobby, really. And an outreach, too."

"An outreach?" the woman asked. "In what way?"

"It might sound grand, but it's my prayer that these tours point folks to the beauty and wonder of nature . . . and most of all, to our great Creator."

The woman nodded her head thoughtfully, then went on to

share that she'd recently left her Ohio Amish community. "It's been difficult to adjust," she said softly. "Not easy to take the Plain life out of a person raised that way. But I won't go back." She glanced over at the man Liz supposed was her boyfriend, who was patiently waiting for her.

"We all must choose how to live," Liz replied, touching the woman's arm. "I'll be sure to remember you in prayer." Then she asked, "Have ya ever heard of Hickory Hollow's Wise Woman, Ella Mae Zook?"

"I think so. Someone's written a book about her, I believe."

Liz gave her Ella Mae's address and encouraged her to go see her. "Just drop by. She's usually available to talk . . . and to pray."

The woman nodded, her tears brimming. "I see compassion in your eyes. Noticed it right away. Keep doing what you're doing, Liz. Today's been a real blessing." She hugged her before heading toward her friend and the parked car.

Matt walked over to Liz, his taxi late in coming. "Everything okay?"

Liz nodded. "She just needed to talk."

"Couldn't help but notice she was payin' close attention to whatever you were saying," Matt replied, eyes serious. "It impressed me, the way ya took time for her like that."

Not used to such directness from a young man she didn't really know, Liz replied, "It's the reason I'm doin' this. To encourage and uplift hearts wherever I can."

"Best way to live," he agreed.

The passenger van pulled up to the curb, and Matt headed toward the back of the carriage to pick up his black grooming tote and empty lunch bag. "See ya next Tuesday, Liz."

"You too," she said, watching him walk away. At the van, Matt turned and waved at her and she waved back. *We're a team, he said. . . .*

8

The next day being an off-Sunday from Preaching, Liz, Martha, and their Mamm bundled up and headed out in the family carriage to visit relatives following a light noon meal. Their first stop was to see Liz's elderly paternal grandparents, who lived a half mile away in their cozy *Dawdi Haus*. Liz's grandmother said she looked forward to spending all day with family on Thanksgiving—"a time to create new memories."

Later, they visited eldest brother, Reuben, and his wife, Gracie, and their family, where Martha Rose read a picture book to the sometimes feisty six-year-old Mary Ruth while Liz played with eighteen-month-old Yonnie, who babbled in *Deitsch* nearly the whole time.

On the return trip, Liz perked up when Mamm mentioned a Bird-in-Hand food pantry that had put out a plea for canned goods. "I heard about it at a quilting frolic yesterday."

Right away, Liz thought of Matt, who'd talked so happily about working at such a place on his days off from buggy tours. *Could it be the same one?*

Matt had also crossed her mind earlier that morning while she was reading from Scripture. *Blessed is he that considereth the poor: the Lord will deliver him in time of trouble*, Psalm forty-one declared.

Should I even be thinking about Matt? Once Adam's home, I won't be seein' him again.

As was her weekly routine, Liz helped Mamm and Martha pin the washing to the clothesline early Monday morning. Although it was only twenty-seven degrees and the clothing would likely freeze, all would be well once they brought the hard, flat items inside to thaw.

Afterward, Liz rolled out enough dough for two pie crusts for the large chicken pot pie Martha was making while Mamm made lemon bars for their dessert. *Mmm, tasty,* Liz thought.

Following the noon meal, Liz hitched Charlie up to the family buggy when Martha Rose was occupied selling eggs to one of their regular customers. Liz was eager to head over to the fabric store in Intercourse Village, one of her favorite places to shop.

Lo and behold, standing in line at the checkout counter was Ashley Hyatt, one of the owners of the Christmas House. Only once before had Liz encountered the woman since the family had moved to Hickory Hollow, a time when Ashley had approached Liz's touring carriage to speak with her briefly.

But Liz didn't try to get Ashley's attention today since customers were milling about—often the case on a Monday afternoon. *While everyone's washing is freeze-drying,* Liz mused, making her way to the shelves of solid-color fabrics, wanting some royal blue material to make a new Sunday dress for herself.

She also needed several yards of faux fur for Mamm, who planned to make a batch of hand muffs for the women riding on the buggy tours during cold snaps like today's frosty weather. Last December, the muffs had been so popular, some customers had asked to purchase them. Surprised at that, Mamm had already increased the number to make this year, something Liz was happy to facilitate.

It didn't take long for Liz to find the dress material she was looking for. From her vantage point, she could still see Ashley, who was just now removing her fleece sports jacket to reveal a pair of skin-tight, lime-green athletic leggings and a matching long-sleeved top. Her face was flushed pink and her brown hair stuck to her temples beneath a black-and-white visor. From the looks of her, Liz assumed she must have ridden to the shop on her bike, a distance of at least three miles.

Just ahead of Ashley in line, two little Amish girls turned suddenly to face her, their eyes opening wide as they looked her over, up and down, openly staring.

They've prob'ly never seen such a getup, thought Liz, feeling sorry for Ashley. *She must feel like a foreigner amidst all these long cape dresses and aprons.*

Ashley simply smiled at the girls. However, before they could react, their mother placed a hand on the older girl's shoulder and moved her forward, speaking firmly in *Deitsch* to both of them. Ashley visibly flinched, not understanding what the Amish mother had said.

Liz clenched her jaw. *Has anyone welcomed Ashley?*

It was earlier than Matt's usual arrival on Tuesday morning when he came into the break room at the hardware store along with Onkel Joe. Surprised, Liz was glad for the company. Joe seemed to have a big talk on, discussing the unusually dry but cold weather. "Still no snow in sight," he said as he poured coffee for the two of them.

"My Dat's been prayin' for moisture," Matt said. "What with the near drought conditions."

After a few minutes of similar small talk, Onkel Joe left the room, and Matt rose for a second cup of coffee. "How were your days off, Liz?" he asked.

She mentioned the Sunday afternoon visit to her Dat's parents, as well as to big brother Reuben and family. "How 'bout yours?"

"We had Preachin' service and stayed for the fellowship meal. Mamm and my three teenage sisters were assigned to help serve and clean up, which meant plenty of time for me to visit with my buddy group out near the stable. Us single guys like to catch up now and then."

"So ya must've had a Singing that evening?" she ventured.

He nodded. "I went for the first half, and after refreshments, I headed home."

She wondered why a nice-lookin' guy like Matt had left early. Wasn't he seeing anyone? "My brother Adam often says the refreshments are the reason he goes!" She smiled. "Well, that and the fellowship. But he can't sing on pitch, which embarrasses him. Poor guy."

"Understandable."

"Singin' off pitch hasn't kept the girls away, though," Liz added before catching herself. She grimaced, but Matt's eyes twinkled. "*Ach*, I shouldn't have said—"

"*Nee*, it's all right, Liz. Say whatever's on your mind."

She was relieved at his response. Now, as she thought about it, there hadn't been any so-called ice to break between them from one touring day to the next, even with a few days off between Saturday and Tuesday. Truth be told, Matt seemed more relaxed around her than even her own brother. And she realized she would miss him once Adam returned.

That Thursday, Liz attended a cousin's wedding with Martha Rose, and they stayed for the feast that followed. Martha's beau was there, too, so Liz returned home alone later that afternoon to spend time with Mamm, who'd been rather quiet lately.

By the light of the gas lamp in the front room, Liz hand-sewed muffs with Mamm, who was sitting in Dat's rocking chair near the black heater stove. As they sewed, Liz tried to encourage her. "Only five weeks or so before Dat and Adam are home again."

Mamm glanced up. "'Tween you an' me, I've been crossin' off the days on my calendar upstairs. We've never been apart for this long."

"I'm sure Dat misses ya, too."

Mamm's eyes turned soft. "I remember when we were courtin', he'd write every other day or so. And we only lived a mile from each other. Ain't that somethin'?"

"That's sweet."

"Even after we wed, your Dat hasn't stopped sayin'—or writin'—how much he loves me." Mamm smiled as she cut a piece of fur for the next muff. "Mind you, he doesn't just say it. He shows his love every day . . . bein' patient and kind."

Liz pondered that for a moment. "If only every girl could marry a man like that."

"Well, I've been prayin' that way for you and Martha Rose, just as I did for your married sisters. The dear Lord has given us such fine sons-in-law, and I believe He'll do the same for our youngest girls."

Hearing this, Liz's heart filled with gratitude and she let her mother's precious words sink deep into her heart. "*Denki*, Mamm. I know you'll keep prayin'."

When Martha Rose arrived home late that night after Ben Fisher dropped her off, Liz tiptoed over to her room. "I have an idea . . . somethin' to cheer up Mamm."

"She *has* been a little blue lately," Martha replied.

"What if we hosted a Sisters Day get-together next Monday afternoon? We could invite Mamm's four sisters and five sisters-in-law, have pie and coffee, and play some table games."

"Sounds perfect," Martha said, taking her hair down and brushing it. "And let's make it a surprise, okay?"

"It'll show how much we all love her."

"I'll get the word out," Martha said, then paused. "Mamm won't be embarrassed 'bout this extra attention, will she?"

"I think she'll enjoy herself. It's been a while since all her sisters and sisters-in-law have been in the same place at the same time. And it'll be nice to have a get-together like this before Thanksgiving."

"I'll bake some dessert bars and a few pies. Hopefully, Mamm won't wonder 'bout that, though. I'll figure out somethin'." Martha set her hairbrush down.

"I can help ya contact Mamm's sisters," Liz offered. "Just want to help Mamm get through 'til Dat's home, ya know? She could use a little encouragement."

Nodding, Martha sat beside Liz on the bed. "I wish I were more like you."

Liz slipped her arm around her. "Well, I think you're just fine—sweet as peppermint taffy."

Later, when Liz was snug beneath her warm handmade bed quilts, she thanked God for a loving, caring mother who devoted time to prayer for the young men who would someday wed her last two daughters living at home. *Mamm's prayers are a gift.*

9

Liz enjoyed going to Friday market the next day, arriving right at nine o'clock when it opened. She, Mamm, and Martha Rose mingled at various market stands, talking with relatives and purchasing items they needed and some Christmas gifts, too. Afterward, they went to a nearby card shop to purchase boxes of Christmas cards. Hearing the carols playing over the intercom made the time there all the more special. Liz could feel the anticipation mount as she thought ahead to the whole family coming home for Christmas dinner, the joyful atmosphere, the smiles and laughter of her dear nephews and nieces, and, of course, Mamm's incredible feast.

Best of all, Dat and Adam will be home!

When they arrived back from shopping, Mamm had a letter from Dat waiting in the mailbox, and Liz couldn't stop smiling about it, wishing Dat could see Mamm's cheerful face. *Her sadness has lifted*, Liz thought, feeling ever so much better for her mother. *Letters from him make all the difference—even more, just maybe, than the Sisters Day gathering will.*

That evening before bedtime in her room, Liz worked on knitting the long, navy-blue scarf, thinking happily of seeing

Matt again tomorrow for the Saturday tours. *He's remarkably good with the tourists and our horse . . . and perty wonderful to work alongside, too,* she thought, knowing she might be just a little biased about the latter.

Following the final tour the next day, Matt waited until all the passengers had driven away, then asked Liz if he could groom King before he left. "Even though I know ya don't want me to bother with it."

This took Liz off guard, and she asked if his driver would be coming at the usual time.

A mischievous smile stretched across his face. "I stepped out on a limb and asked him to come an hour later than usual."

What on earth? Liz was taken aback. "*Ach*, there's no need to groom King by yourself when *I* can help," she said, then laughed a little when Matt opened his trusty grooming tote and handed her the dandy brush.

Liz worked on King's long, regal neck while Matt removed the trapped debris from the right front hoof, working from heel to toe. As he did so, he spoke softly to the horse. *Like the smithy does.*

The sun was near the western horizon now, though the sky was still filled with light. Several buggies drove past as the two of them worked, and one family buggy slowed up considerably.

Looking toward the road, Liz could see Martha Rose at the reins and Mamm seated next to her. Mamm waved as Martha smiled and nodded her head, both of them surely getting a good, long look at Matt.

Liz returned the wave. *Are they really that curious about Adam's replacement?*

"You must know those folks." Matt glanced up at her while holding the horse's right back hoof between his knees.

"That was my Mamm and my youngest sister."

Matt nodded. "So you have at least one sister and one brother that I know of."

"*Jah*, Adam and Martha Rose. But I also have two married brothers and two married sisters." She looked down and noted that he was doing a thorough job. "I understand from my Dat there are nine children in *your* family."

"My Mamm's always said a big family makes for the most fun. And Dat says sticks in a bundle are hard to break." Matt moved to work on the back left hoof as she shifted to the opposite side.

"Do you have school-age siblings?" she asked, recalling his patient way with the children on the tours.

"The youngest are triplet boys who just turned six."

"Triplets? Your Mamm must've had some help when they were babies."

"Actually, she assigned a baby to each of my three sisters once the triplets were weaned. But immediately after their births, both my *Grossmammi* came and spent a lot of time at our house for the first few weeks. Dat helped, too. He's always helped, 'specially with our little ones, and he cooks to give Mamm a break from kitchen work."

Liz was impressed. "I don't know many husbands who cook."

Matt explained that his Dat's father—Dawdi Yoder—had been the same way with his big family, changing diapers and playing with the toddlers and cooking. "Like father, like son, I guess. Believe it or not, I've learned a lot 'bout cooking and even kitchen tips from both my parents," Matt continued. "I mean, a guy should know how to survive on his own, right?"

Liz tittered. *That's rare around here.*

Soon, they were talking about whatever came to mind, Matt asking her more about her family and herself. "I'm guessin' you're baptized," he said at one point.

She nodded. "My baptismal day was . . . well, I'm not sure I can even describe it." She remembered the moment the bishop had placed his water-filled hands on her head as though it was just yesterday. "I can say that it was precious and holy, for certain. My heart was filled with such peace, even joy."

Matt stopped the hoof picking and stood up. "That's just beautiful, Liz." Their eyes met briefly. "Never heard it said quite that way."

Now Liz had to know. "Have you joined church, too?"

"*Jah*, and like you, I literally felt God's presence that day. It's difficult to put into words other than to say the air seemed thicker somehow with His blessing."

She wanted to soak up Matt's response, her heart was so moved. "I truly understand."

Goodness, the more she learned about Matt, the more she wanted to know. There were so many questions she wanted to ask him. And all the way home, she pondered just how easy it was to talk openly with him.

It was close to dark by the time Liz arrived home that Saturday evening. She led King to the stable, where the stalls had been mucked out and fresh bedding straw put down. *Reuben and Henry were here*, she thought, grateful for their help.

She returned to the house and washed up, and as Liz might have expected, Martha Rose got things off to an interesting start at the table after Mamm asked the silent blessing. "I noticed ya had some extra help groomin' King today," Martha said, trying to keep a straight face.

"And *I* noticed yous rode by."

Mamm remained silent, politely forking up some green beans with ham bits from her plate.

"Thought ya didn't want Matt to do that," Martha continued, unable to squelch her smile now.

"I didn't."

"Well, but there he was, groomin' to beat the band . . . and with your help, too."

"True."

Martha rolled her eyes. "Okay, if ya don't wanna talk 'bout it . . ."

"*Ach*, girls, such a conversation," Mamm teased with an exaggerated roll of her eyes.

Liz reached for the tuna noodle casserole and dished it up. "I'll fill you in later, Martha, never fear."

Martha Rose gave a conspiratorial wink and laughed. "I'll count on it."

10

Once Mamm retired to her room for the evening, Liz was amazed to learn from her sister the lengths she had gone to that day, preparing for Mamm's upcoming surprise gathering. Reuben's wife, Gracie, had come by to pick Mamm up for much of the day, and while Liz had been busy with Saturday tours, Martha Rose had secretly baked all the goodies, as well as aired out the kitchen before Mamm's return. She'd even wrapped up and hidden the pies and chocolate bars downstairs in the cold cellar to keep them fresh.

Liz wished she'd been able to do more than just contact some of Mamm's sisters and make sure the kitchen and front room were redded up. "You're really determined for this to be a surprise," she said. And Martha assured her that the Sisters Day get-together had something in store beyond just some cheering up and eating baked goods.

"You'll see," Martha told her with a sly expression on her pretty face.

Snow flurries seemed to hang in the air as they floated down, and they continued through Monday breakfast and the noon meal. Strangely, Mamm kept looking out the kitchen windows as she swept the floor while Martha and Liz washed and dried the dishes.

"According to the paper, there won't be any snow accumulation," Liz told Mamm. "Reuben and Henry should easily be able to get here to work in the barn."

"I sure hope so," Mamm replied. Her hair came to a slight widow's peak beneath her pressed white prayer Kapp, and she looked well rested. Liz noted she was wearing her plum-colored dress and black cape and apron.

Why is Mamm dressed up?

Mamm's eldest sister, sixty-four-year-old Nellie Ann, was the first to arrive that afternoon, carrying a large wicker basket of craft items—ribbons and small spools of wire and whatnot. Her white-gray hair was accentuated by her black dress, cape, and long apron. Fortunately, Mamm was upstairs when she arrived, and Liz and Martha Rose welcomed their aunt into the utility room, where she hung up her black coat, scarf, and outer bonnet.

Shortly after, the rest of the sisters and sisters-in-law came in, all of them having parked their buggies behind the barn, out of sight. Quickly, Martha Rose ushered all nine of them into the front room, where they sat as silent as the snow in their best black or blue dresses, capes, and aprons.

When Mamm descended the stairs, they all called out, "Surprise!" with Nellie Ann clapping and grinning.

Mamm smiled sweetly, then started to laugh when she spotted the wicker basket holding red and green decorations. "Ain't Christmas already . . . is it?"

This brought titters all around.

"Thought we could have a nice time makin' candle rings for

ourselves for Christmas," Nellie Ann offered, smiling at Liz. "And some extras, as well."

Ah, the surprise Martha hinted about, thought Liz, delighted indeed.

Martha excused herself to go and put several leaves in the kitchen table, since doing so earlier would have spoiled the surprise. Mamm's two younger sisters made haste to join her in the kitchen.

The afternoon was filled with happy interactions, talk of Thanksgiving plans and the annual Christmas program at the schoolhouse, as well as generous servings of Martha Rose's pies and chocolate bars. Each woman seemed to enjoy creating two red-and-green-ribboned candle rings with *Aendi* Nellie Ann's instructions, and some made more for gifts. Meanwhile, Mamm seemed none the wiser as to the real reason for the get-together.

Liz did notice there were a few hushed remarks about the Christmas House and all the commotion already going on over there. "Just think of the backup on the roads yet again," someone grumbled.

"The more decorations, the less focus on Christ," declared another.

Uneasy, Liz tried not to listen.

That evening, Liz and Martha Rose talked privately in Liz's room, glad Mamm hadn't asked any questions about the homemade pies and sweet bars, or why only her close female relatives had come over.

"It wonders me why Mamm dressed up, though," Liz said.

"Maybe she was tipped off, but who'd want to spoil the surprise?"

"It was such a nice time, and Mamm's spirits were lifted. That's what matters." Liz paused. "It's possible she *did* know ahead of time and played along so none of us would be disappointed."

"Hard to say." Martha hugged her. "Sweet dreams, sister."

After Martha left the room, Liz picked up the pretty candle rings she'd made, turning them over and admiring them. *Christmastime will soon be here*, she thought, knowing how bustling the local Amish shops would become, as well as her own buggy tour business.

She unpinned her bun and let her chestnut-brown hair fall to her waist, brushed it for a while, then dressed for bed. She outened the gas lamp and slipped under the quilts, then said her silent rote prayer, ending with a request for Dat and Adam's safe return . . . and for God to reveal His plan for her life.

I yearn to know Thy will, O Lord.

On her way to work the Tuesday before Thanksgiving, Liz wondered how she would feel seeing Matt. *After our visit last time, does he still think of me merely as a coworker?*

She directed King into the parking lot with the touring carriage and saw Matt sitting in the wood structure. As usual, his insulated lunch bag and the black grooming tote were at his side. He waved and got up to come over to her.

"You're early," she said, tying the horse to the hitching post.

He chuckled. "So are you."

Last Saturday, we arrived early and stayed later, she thought, falling into step with him as they headed toward the hardware store. In the break room, they had coffee, and Onkel Joe popped his head in to say "hullo" but didn't stay around.

"I discovered somethin' interesting, Liz." Matt took a sip of his coffee. "My Dat told me that we're related to one of your preachers here in Hickory Hollow."

"Must be Preacher Yoder," she replied as she stirred sugar into her coffee. "He's in his eighties by now, I think, but he still preaches occasionally. He can't stand for too long anymore."

"Turns out he's Dat's cousin somewhere down the line." Matt drank more of his coffee, then set his mug down. "A fine, godly man who has only *gut* things to say 'bout your church district."

"Well, it's a *gut* place to live," she said. "And apart from the hubbub over the Hyatts' Christmas decorations, we're a fairly contented bunch."

"Speakin' of that, the first buggy tour to the Christmas House is comin' up soon." Matt's eyes brightened.

Liz nodded. "My cousin Roy says the Christmas tour reservations are nearly full."

By the time they finished their coffees and headed outdoors, two cars were already parked in the lot, so Liz picked up her pace. *Ach, we lost track of time talking . . . again.*

The day seemed to fly by, and with the holiday near at hand, passengers were especially curious about Amish Thanksgiving traditions. Liz explained that she and her family either attended a wedding on Thanksgiving Day or enjoyed a big meal and spent the afternoon playing board games and singing together. "But the main focus is on giving gratitude to God for the bountiful harvest and for every small blessing, too."

Without missing a beat, Matt added, "Some of my Amish relatives in Clark, Missouri, attend church on Thanksgiving Day. Other groups in different states have a benefit dinner to raise money for their schools."

Liz appreciated his contribution. "I know of Amish in Kentucky who have a Widows Supper on Thanksgiving evening, which I think is real nice," she said.

Momentarily, the passengers talked quietly amongst themselves before one of them asked, "Is turkey the main Thanksgiving entrée for an Amish family?"

Liz said it was. "Actually, Thanksgiving and Christmas dinners are very similar, and a lot of the side dishes and desserts we serve would be like what your families enjoy—mashed potatoes and gravy, and pumpkin or pecan pie for dessert. Some of my dessert favorites are angel food cake and homemade Reese's bars."

Glancing at her, Matt joked, "Anybody hungry?"

The passengers laughed, and a woman said, "How can I get invited to an Amish Thanksgiving dinner?"

"There are Amish folk in the area who offer dinners in their homes for a price," Liz said, "just not on Thanksgiving, as you can understand."

"Is that information found online?" the woman asked.

"*Jah*, just go to the Discover Lancaster website." Liz always felt funny about sharing such things, as if she were well-versed in the cyber world. *Quite the opposite!*

Matt gave her an encouraging smile, and she soaked it right up.

11

Thanksgiving Day dawned with brilliance, nary a cloud in the sky. Liz imagined Dat must be thankful for the rather dry weather in Pennsylvania all these weeks, making it possible for the house expansion to move forward to completion. *Maybe he can come home sooner*, she thought, torn between wanting that especially for Mamm's sake . . . and knowing it would mean losing touch with Matt. For surely Adam would return to helping her with the buggy tours again.

Reuben and Gracie had invited Mamm and the immediate family, as well as Dat's parents, for Thanksgiving dinner at noon, when everyone would sit around their twelve-foot-long table. Gracie had stuffed and baked two large turkeys for the feast and made numerous side dishes, and Liz's two married sisters had brought some sides, as well. For dessert, there were more pies and other goodies than the long kitchen counter could hold, so another folding table was brought up from the basement to accommodate all the food in the spacious kitchen.

Liz's young nephews and nieces played in one corner of the kitchen, and two toddlers had hidden under the table. Martha Rose spied them and managed to coax them out just before everyone gathered to sit down.

There was enough food for seconds, and eighty-seven-year-old Dawdi Lantz hinted at wanting some leftover turkey to take home "for a sandwich later, just maybe." Gracie assured him there'd be plenty for that, and Dawdi reached for her hand and squeezed it.

Mammi Lantz looked so contented sitting at the table and holding her sleeping three-month-old granddaughter. She bowed her head for the silent table blessing led by Reuben at the far end of the table. After the prayer, when the baby whimpered, Mammi reluctantly gave her back to her mother. Observing this, Liz tried to imagine holding her own little one someday, and a sweet longing filled her heart.

After the meal and all the dishes, pots, and pans were washed, wiped, and put away, everyone assembled in the front room for a time of singing songs of thanksgiving. Later, the family divided up to play various games—Farm-opoly, Dutch Blitz, Uno, and Scrabble.

There were fewer family members at the early supper hours later, since some of the siblings had plans to visit in-laws, wanting to see both sides of the family on this special day. Liz was happy to linger at Reuben's to spend more time with Gracie and their two playful children.

By the time Mamm talked of heading home, twilight had fallen. Liz offered to take the driving lines, since Mamm had trouble seeing after sunset. As they rode, Mamm fell quiet, surely thinking of Dat, and Liz found herself thinking of Matt, wondering about his day with family.

Driving past the Hyatts' farmhouse and yard, Liz could see the familiar trappings all set up and ready to go, the decorative lights still dark. *Tomorrow they'll flip the switch and light up the whole place*, she thought with a rush of excitement, looking forward to the first buggy tour to the Christmas House this Saturday afternoon.

It'll be nice to have Matt along this year. Even more so than Adam, she thought before catching herself.

During a simple breakfast of homemade granola with bananas and coffee the next morning, Mamm suggested they go to the general store and purchase a box of canned goods to donate to the food pantry she'd heard about.

Liz eagerly agreed.

"I'll call for a driver to pick us up and bring us home," Mamm said, indicating that she didn't want to take the horse and buggy clear over to Bird-in-Hand.

"We could prob'ly donate some of our own canned goods—we have so many," Martha Rose said, referring to their shelves of pantry items down cellar.

"Accordin' to the flyer, they don't accept home-canned goods," Mamm told her.

"So off to the general store we go," Liz said. "It's much closer than goin' all the way to Quarryville to BB's Grocery Outlet, then backtracking to Bird-in-Hand."

When they arrived at the food pantry, Liz was surprised at the many cars parked out front. "Folks must be helpin' to restock the items distributed before Thanksgiving," she said.

"Which is why I waited 'til today to come," Mamm replied.

"*Gut* idea," Martha Rose said as she slid the side door open on the passenger van.

The driver went around to the back and lifted out the box of canned goods they'd purchased earlier, offering to carry it for Mamm.

Inside, Liz saw Plain and English folk alike donating canned and boxed foods, as well as paper products. The store was well organized with shelves for pastas, beans, and jarred and canned goods that included soups, vegetables, and peanut butter. A sight to behold. And although she had no idea before arriving if this was the same place where Matt volunteered, within a few minutes, she spotted him pushing a grocery cart for an elderly gentleman using a walker. Seeing Matt there doing what he loved warmed her heart. She remembered what he'd said about this being a practical kind of ministry.

When Mamm was ready to leave, Liz heard her name called, and when she turned to look, Matt was walking toward her.

"Well, this is a surprise!" He smiled broadly.

She greeted him and explained that her Mamm had seen a flyer and come to donate canned goods. "That's why we're here."

"Ah, so you're *not* stalkin' me." He winked.

She chuckled at his little joke. "Would ya like to meet my Mamm . . . and my sister Martha Rose?" she asked, knowing they both would enjoy it very much.

"Sure would."

Liz found it easy to introduce them to Matt, and he to them. She felt proud of her friendship with him, almost as if she were showing him off to her family. Mamm brightened when she learned who he was and asked how long he'd been volunteering there. Martha simply stood back and observed, giving Liz an occasional sideways glance. Liz got the impression that Martha was trying to hold it together, seeing Matt talk with their mother like this.

During the ride home in the van, Liz could almost feel Martha's eagerness to share her thoughts, yet amazingly, her sister was able to keep still for the entire trip back to Hickory Hollow.

But while Mamm was paying the driver, Martha grabbed Liz's hand and hurried them toward the back porch. "You never told me he was so *handsome*."

"Well, his looks weren't the first thing I noticed," Liz blurted in response, although she felt heat creep into her face.

Martha was blinking like crazy. "Are ya kiddin' me?"

Liz had to laugh and explained quietly as they made their way into the house that it was Matt's kind manner that initially caught her attention. "Not how nice-lookin' he is."

"Well, this has to be a first." Martha shook her head.

Liz assumed Martha was thinking of her former beau, who was also very good-looking, a fact that had not been lost on either Liz or Martha when he and Liz had started going out. "I hope I've matured since Calvin, dear sister. I can tell ya there's far more than meets the eye when it comes to Matt Yoder."

Martha washed her hands at the kitchen sink, glancing over at her several times. "Do ya hear yourself?" She dried her hands and leaned back against the sink. "Not only do I think Matt's sweet on ya, but I wonder if *you* might not be fallin' for him, too."

Liz shrugged, embarrassed, but it wasn't as simple as that. "I really don't know," she replied.

Mamm entered the kitchen just then, and Liz was relieved to see her, since it was time to make the noon meal anyway. All the while, Martha's comments lingered in her mind.

Saturday's dawning shone on the fresh dusting of snow as Liz opened her dark green window shades. "First day of the Christmas House buggy tours," she murmured, stretching her arms and yawning.

Last night, before falling asleep, she'd thought a lot about her and Martha's curious conversation. What had her sister so quickly seen between Liz and Matt that she hadn't? Surely it wasn't Matt's winking at her with his joke. Even Dat winked when he was teasing them. Was it Matt's easygoing manner with

Mamm as they talked? Yet Liz knew from experience that Matt was that way around everyone.

Sitting at the window and staring down at the pastureland, Liz realized that a person could actually take Matt's comments and actions two ways. Being ultra-friendly and engaging might just be how Dat had asked him to be while on the buggy tours with her. On the other hand, Liz could sort of see how Martha Rose might have mistaken Matt's friendliness at the food pantry as potential romantic interest.

At last, it was time for the final buggy tour of the day to begin, the one Liz had been anticipating for weeks. The earlier skiff of snow had disappeared due to the mild temperature—even the sky had a softness to it. Her passengers seemed delighted with the buggy ride past farmhouses and vast fields, chatting and laughing with her and sometimes Matt during their commentary.

At the Amish Toy Store, many of them lined up at the cash register to purchase the wooden cars, trucks, doll cradles, and doll-sized rocking chairs. Being Amish-owned, the shop was not decorated for Christmas, but there was a vibrant expectation in the air now that Thanksgiving Day was behind them and Christmas was less than a month away.

Spirits on the buggy ride to the Christmas House were festive, and the Hyatts' music was loud enough to hear quite a distance away. As they came upon the lit-up display, the passengers pointed to the dancing elves, but the main attraction was the large rooftop Santa in his reindeer-drawn sleigh. Matt looked her way, sort of shrugging at the spectacular show as the younger children in the buggy squealed with delight.

It's just so strange to see in the middle of Amish farmland and houses, she thought.

She didn't dwell on this, though, wanting instead to share about family traditions as she halted the horse in front of the Christmas House. "We Amish don't decorate like our English neighbors here, but we have our own ways of celebrating the Lord's birthday. Every Christmas for as long as I remember, my Mamm has served baked oatmeal with maple syrup and cinnamon for breakfast, and pancakes with strawberries and whipped cream."

"Yum!" one little boy interjected enthusiastically.

"Then, after breakfast, we all stay around the table while my Dat opens the Good Book and reads from chapter two of the Gospel of Luke, about the Lord's birth in a stable surrounded by cattle. I love that passage because it tells how Mary and Joseph were so far from their home and family, and weary from travelin'—poor Mary, great with child, on a donkey—yet they trusted in God to provide," Liz told them. "At the end of that reading, Dat always reminds us, 'The Lord Jesus left the glories of heaven to bring us hope and healing. Never forget.'"

The tour guests' murmured responses sounded like a soft hum. This had been Liz's favorite story to tell last December during the Christmas House Buggy Tour. And she felt the honest beauty and hope of it once again.

Continuing, she said, "The day before Christmas Eve, we head to the Amish schoolhouse for the annual program. This year, my six-year-old niece will be in the nativity play as one of the angels. And let me tell ya, she doesn't quite fit the part . . . ornery as she is."

A peal of laughter followed.

Liz went on to talk about the popular traditions of exchanging cookies and decorating the house with simple garlands of Christmas cards hanging over the entrances to the kitchen and the front room. "And along with some evergreen cuttings on the table, my Mamm will set out white tapers in candle rings with red-and-green ribbons," she added, remembering the fun of making the candle rings at her mother's Sisters Day gathering.

A man wearing a Phillies ball cap and matching jersey wanted to ask a question. "I realize Santa Claus doesn't play a part in Amish celebrations, but do you give each other presents?"

"Absolutely, 'specially to the children. Some Amish families make all their gifts; others purchase them or give a mixture of both."

Another person raised a hand. "What do the Amish neighbors think of having this noisy and decorated-to-the-hilt house in the middle of their quiet village?"

Liz drew a quick breath, wanting to keep a positive mood in the carriage and not really sure what to say since her seasonal buggy tours made the house a highlight yet added to the traffic in the area. She looked over at Matt.

Graciously, he took the cue. "I know the owner of this farmhouse," he said. "And truly, the man just wants to demonstrate all the Christmas joy and beauty he can for his family and the community. Spreadin' joy is his only goal."

Matt hadn't really answered the passenger's question, but what he'd said kept things light and cheerful, the way Liz had hoped. She was thankful again for his quick thinking and tact.

She directed the horse slowly toward the large nativity scene on the other side of the yard. "Here's my favorite part of the display," she told the passengers. "Just look at all those angels in that heavenly choir."

"The background music makes ya want to join in with 'Hark! The Herald Angels Sing,' doesn't it?" Matt said, smiling at her again.

A few passengers did start to sing along, quietly at first, then with more gusto, a delight to hear. And Liz hoped nothing more would be asked about the brilliantly lit farmhouse that stood out so boldly amongst its Plain neighbors.

At Ella Mae's, a variety of Christmas cookies on trays and cups of hot cocoa with marshmallows waited just inside the back door when Liz and Matt brought the passengers up to the back porch.

"*Willkumm*, everyone! Can yous sing for your treats?" Ella Mae joked from where she stood in the doorway, her face crinkling into a smile. "A Christmas carol will do."

Liz wasn't expecting this since Ella Mae hadn't done this last year—a woman full of surprises, for sure.

Matt quickly led out in "Joy to the World," and everyone joined in while Liz began to bring out the cookie trays before going back for the hot cocoa.

All the while, the Wise Woman bobbed her little head as they sang, her black shawl wrapped around her slight shoulders. Liz couldn't wait to visit her another time for tea, just the two of them, but for now, she enjoyed the special moment there on Ella Mae's porch.

12

The next week's tours were lively and fun, even the ones that weren't seasonal. Now that it was December, passengers had started showing up in festive sweaters, holiday-themed jewelry, and even a few in red stocking caps, demonstrating Christmas spirit.

After wrapping up the final tour of the week, Liz and Matt groomed the horse together yet again, and Liz thanked him for sticking around, and for his pleasant, easy way with the customers. "They really like ya, Matt," she said, blushing that he might think she was including herself.

"No need to thank me, Liz," he said as he picked the debris out of King's hoof. "I'm enjoying it." He stood up just then. "Tell ya what, though. We can talk more 'bout the tours over coffee and pie on Monday afternoon, if you'd like. I'll send a driver for ya around two o'clock and meet ya at the Bird-in-Hand Bakery and Cafe. Okay?"

She had not seen this invitation coming and was speechless . . . and felt strangely shy. But why? She knew Matt well enough, and they'd clicked early on while working together.

Is this a date? Am I ready to go out with him?

"S'pose I'll need your address," Matt said with a smile.

"Uh . . . *jah*, of course." She told him where the driver should pick her up. "Nice of you."

"I'm looking forward to it." He was outright grinning now.

Liz's thoughts were racing as they finished grooming King, and later, too, as she headed home in the carriage. *Wait till Martha hears 'bout this!*

Liz's wind-up clock alarm jingled her awake the next morning, and immediately, she was alert. She'd told Martha the surprising news about Matt last night. "*How do you feel about him?*" Martha had asked. And Liz still grappled with the question, curious as to why she'd felt so shy around Matt after he'd asked her out.

What am I worried about? I've spent plenty-a time with him lately. It's just a casual get-together.

There was one thing Liz knew for sure: She must go and visit Ella Mae Zook. And very soon.

That morning at the Preaching service held at Onkel Joe's farmhouse, Liz was distracted and fidgeted in her seat, especially when Preacher Yoder rose to give the first of the usual two sermons—the first sermon being the shorter. Seeing the elderly man speak to the congregation pushed her thoughts back to Matt. *Why did he tell me about his Dat's relationship to our minister?*

Preacher Yoder asked the People to pray that his words would be wholly directed by the Lord, something the ordained brethren always humbly requested.

Liz studied him, looking for a physical resemblance to Matt, and as she observed him, listening closely, she detected a similarity. Not so much a physical one, though. The theme of his sermon was kindness—going out of one's way for another, and Preacher Yoder recited the biblical account of the Good Samaritan from the Gospel of Luke.

During the sermon, Liz imagined Matt being the Samaritan man who helped the wounded Jewish man lying on the road.

"The Samaritan was not fearful of helping the injured man who was of a different background," said Preacher Yoder. "*Nee*, he set aside the potential shame and ignored the social customs of the time to reach out to his neighbor. In other words, the Samaritan chose to do what was right in God's eyes."

It sure seemed like Preacher Yoder was trying to get the congregation to focus on something practical. Something, just maybe, that was a sore spot in the middle of their own community, now that traffic had returned to the roads near the Christmas House. At least that's how Liz took it. On the other hand, if she was mistaken in her assumption, the message of the sermon was still very clear. They were to show compassion to those outside their Plain circles.

After the sermon, Liz and everyone in attendance turned and knelt at the benches to pray silently where they'd been sitting. And Liz asked God to show her ways to demonstrate kindness to everyone, even outsiders.

When Liz gathered after the service with Martha Rose and their cousins Fran and Naomi at the far end of the backyard, Fran whispered that she thought the first sermon might be a "hard pill to swallow" for a lot of folks around here. "I mean, think 'bout it."

Martha Rose looked befuddled. "How hard is it to be kind to others?"

Fran quickly filled Martha Rose in on what she'd determined to be the point of the first sermon, confirming Liz's own suspicions. "One of my Bruders—I won't say which one—said last night at supper that somethin' bad's gonna happen what with all the cars comin' to see the Christmas House, and the Englishers' disregard for horses and buggies."

Hearing this, Liz shivered.

"Maybe one of the lanes in the road could be blocked off to make it impossible for cars to return the way they came in? If that happened, ya'd have to drive past the Christmas House an' keep goin' to get to another crossroad," Fran suggested.

Liz wondered how that could work, since doing so would take cars—and buggies—far out of their way . . . and just for a glimpse of the light and music display.

"Sounds like a detour to me," Naomi declared. "Which would definitely discourage outsiders from coming at all."

"Isn't that too much of an all-or-nothin' approach?" Martha Rose asked. "Besides, the buggies passin' by are just tryin' to get home for milkin'."

Liz said nothing, thinking that Fran's and Naomi's families must be influencing the girls' strong opinions. And, too, if the road were partially closed, there'd be no way to get Liz's customers back to Ella Mae's for cookies and hot cocoa to end the Christmas House Buggy Tour before dark.

Sighing, Liz felt torn yet again.

On this very mild December Sunday, the older folks began to move toward the back porch as the first seating for the fellowship meal commenced indoors. Liz spotted Ella Mae in the midst of them, leaning on her daughter Mattie Beiler's right arm.

"Excuse me," Liz told her sister and cousins before hurrying across the yard to the Wise Woman.

"Hullo there, Lizzy," Ella Mae said when she saw her.

Liz stepped close to speak softly. "Just wondered if ya'll be home this afternoon?"

"I will, indeed." Ella Mae's eyes caught hers. "And I'll put a kettle on, dearie."

Smiling with relief, Liz thanked her and turned to head back to Martha Rose and their cousins. Knowing she could talk with Ella Mae before tomorrow's coffee date with Matt made her feel somewhat better.

On the buggy ride home, Liz noticed a number of church members and their families walking toward their farms.

"A great day to be outdoors," Martha Rose said. "'Specially after sittin' in church all mornin'."

Mamm was deep in thought at the reins, not replying.

Later, after they arrived home and Mamm was getting ready to unhitch Charlie, Liz asked, "Might I take the buggy out this afternoon?"

"Help yourself," Mamm said, and Liz hurried into the barn to get some hay for Charlie to munch on.

The day felt almost balmy as Liz headed toward Ella Mae's. Lowering the window on the driver's side, she breathed in the fresh air, the breeze brushing her face. The landscape looked lonely, stark and brown as it was, awaiting a real snow, not a mere dusting. *Where is winter?*

Just ahead on the left side of the road, Liz could see a runner pausing to take a breather—a slender woman in pale-blue-and-black jogging pants and a matching top. *Is that Ashley Hyatt?*

Liz slowed the horse, as the carriage was nearly parallel with the woman now. Then, catching sight of her face, Liz pulled the horse over onto the shoulder and waved. "Would ya like a ride?" she called.

There was no hesitation on Ashley's part as she immediately crossed the road. "Thanks, I think I outran my endurance," she said, getting in on the left side of the buggy. "It's Liz, right?"

"*Jah*, and it's nice to see ya again, Ashley." Picking up the driving lines, Liz eased the horse back onto the road.

"So this is what the inside of an Amish buggy looks like."

"It's surprisingly small, ain't so?" Liz glanced at her. "How far'd ya run?"

Ashley adjusted her headband and looked at the gadget on her left arm. "Let's see. According to my fitness tracker, seven miles . . . and obviously I'm not even home yet."

"That *is* a long way."

"For some reason, it seemed longer today."

Liz stayed quiet, hoping the woman might keep talking.

"Not that I'm complaining," Ashley said. "I enjoy running or biking every day, especially when our three children are in school or out with Logan, like today. They're Christmas shopping. And since cold weather is bound to come at some point, I'm making an effort to get outdoors as much as possible."

Seeing an opening there, Liz asked, "How old are your children?"

"Dalton's thirteen. Bella is eleven, going on eighteen." Ashley laughed. "And Jace is nine."

"Hope ya don't mind me askin', but how do they like livin' in the country?" Liz purposely did not say *amongst the Amish.*

"Oh, is *that* ever a story." Ashley seemed to settle back in the bench seat. "Before we moved here, Logan and I both found ourselves caught up in the New Jersey tech world. He was an IT manager, and I was an information security analyst." She told

Liz that they both woke up one day and felt they were losing precious time with their children. "We wanted a totally different lifestyle. So we looked online for the ideal little farm, with no luck. Then, one day while driving around Lancaster County, we stumbled onto Hickory Hollow, unaware it even existed. Of course, everyone thought we were out of our minds to leave the big city to move to the so-called boonies and work remotely in lower-paying jobs. But we craved the idea of getting our hands in the soil, growing some of our food, and giving our children a more peaceful life, which they're slowly becoming accustomed to . . . and enjoying, too."

Liz caught herself nodding her head. "I know what ya mean 'bout living in the hollow. It's hard to find if ya don't know where it is. And it's a *wunnerbaar-gut* place to bring up children."

Ashley was quiet for a time. Then she spoke again. "Thank goodness, our children have been quite resilient through this big change. But they love having a large property to explore and help garden. They're enjoying their schools, too, which is a real plus." She paused. "I do wonder what our neighbors think of us, though. We don't really know any of them, since we're rather new to the area." She smiled at Liz. "It still seems . . . a bit lonely, I guess," she said more softly.

Pausing, she looked out the window, then toward Liz. "I remember when we had electricity installed last year, some of the buggies would slow down in front of our house, and the Amish folks inside just stared . . . like they couldn't believe it." She shook her head and sighed. "Except for a couple of people like you, we haven't been very warmly received."

Liz was sorry to hear that but didn't reveal that she knew why there was standoffishness. *Undoubtedly it's mostly due to the chaos the Christmas House has brought to the community.*

"Maybe people are still getting used to the idea of your house no longer being owned by Amish after so many generations," Liz mentioned gingerly. "And it must be a challenge for you to live close to folks who look and act like they're straight out of an old-fashioned storybook," she added, trying to sympathize.

"Well, I actually adore waking up to the sound of horses' hooves on the road and the clatter of the carriages. It's beyond quaint," Ashley said. "The definition of tranquility."

Liz made the turn toward the Hyatts' farm and slowed the horse's gait.

Ashley squinted now at the Christmas display. "My husband wants to add even more outdoor lights."

"This year?" Liz reacted without thinking.

Nodding, Ashley replied, "He's determined to have the biggest and best display in Lancaster County."

Liz was surprised Ashley was telling her this. "Well now . . . that is somethin'."

Ashley waved her hand dismissively. "You're so sweet to give me a ride." She smiled. "Thank you, Liz."

"Happy to help. Have yourself a relaxin' afternoon . . . now that you've had your long run, that is!"

The woman got out of the buggy and waved, then hurried toward the festooned house.

Well, what about that? Liz had enjoyed hearing how it was that Ashley and her family had come to live here.

Still mulling over Ashley's revealing comments, she signaled the horse to a trot and looked forward to sipping some delicious peppermint tea with Ella Mae.

13

Liz directed the horse around to the back of Ella Mae's little *Dawdi Haus* and halted beside the black hitching post. Over yonder on the square white porch, Ella Mae was leaning on the banister to peer at her barren flower bed.

"Hullo," Liz called as she tied up the horse.

"So glad ya came." Ella Mae smiled as Liz moved up the walkway. "Have ya ever known of crocuses to start poppin' up in December?" At Liz's shake of the head, the Wise Woman added, "To be safe, I had one of my grandsons lay extra mulch on this patch yesterday."

Liz nodded. "That'll keep them toasty once cold weather comes."

"Only the Good Lord knows when that'll be, 'cause the weatherman sure doesn't." Ella Mae turned toward the back door. "Let's go in an' have us a nice cup of tea."

Liz waited for her to take the lead, then followed, already glad she'd come.

Inside the back door, the small kitchen was sunlit and cheery. The small table was already set with placemats, teacups and saucers, and utensils, just the way Ella Mae liked it. She was always ready to invite someone in for tea without having to rush around, giving her more time to listen.

When the peppermint tea was poured and the ceramic honey container placed on the table, Ella Mae sat across from Liz and bowed her head. "*Denki*, dear Lord, for sendin' Lizzy to me this afternoon. Bless our time together and this warm tea. I pray this in Thy Son's holy name. Amen."

Hearing her pray so sweetly touched Liz, making her feel even calmer.

Ella Mae offered her some honey for her tea, which Liz accepted. "I also have banana bread and a few cookies, too, if you'd like."

"*Denki*, but I ate myself full at the fellowship meal after church."

"It was a light meal, but I did, too. The schnitz pie was too *gut* for chust one piece." Ella Mae tittered merrily.

Liz nodded, and they sipped their tea and made small talk.

Ella Mae commented on two weddings she'd attended recently. "I seem to relive my own weddin' vows near every time." Her eyes moistened. "But let's talk 'bout whatever's on *your* mind, dearie. Surely that's why you're here?"

Liz forced a smile. "Honestly, I've been nervous 'bout a date I have tomorrow afternoon."

Ella Mae's soft blue eyes looked thoughtful. "Nervous, ya say?"

Liz explained her working relationship with Matt, his overall kindness and big-heartedness, even his wisdom. "But a strange shyness came over me when he asked me out."

"'Twas a surprise, then?"

"*Jah*, even though we've been workin' together these past weeks. In my thinkin', that's all it was." She sighed. "But Martha Rose was certain almost immediately that he was interested in me."

"Does she know Matt?"

"*Nee*, she's only met him once. Based just on what I've been tellin' her 'bout working with him. Somehow, she connected the dots before I did."

Ella Mae set down her teacup on its saucer. "Have ya been thinking it's time for a new relationship, maybe?"

"Well, I *have* been hopin' to meet someone, but I'm befuddled 'bout my reaction to Matt's invitation."

Ella Mae took her time replying, gazing out the window like she was thinking. At last, she said gently, "Could it be that you're lookin' at him through different eyes now that ya realize he's not just a coworker, but a potential beau?"

Liz nodded. This made so much sense. "I've actually caught myself feelin' drawn to him at times, but I've tried not to get ahead of myself."

"Why's that, dearie?" Ella Mae poured more tea for them.

Liz shrugged. "Maybe I'm just hesitant to get involved with another guy after my previous breakup, even though it was mutual." She inhaled slowly. "Thing is, I put up boundaries with Matt because we were workin' together so well. I didn't want to lose the friendship we've been enjoying."

Ella Mae reached across the table and squeezed Liz's hand. "Trustin' people can sometimes be *gut* practice for trustin' God."

Liz blinked back tears. Never before had she heard this.

"If you've been gettin' on so well, I daresay you'll have yourself a nice time with this young man tomorrow, honey-girl."

Liz picked up her dainty teacup and sipped some more tea. "I hope so."

"Remember, Lizzy, *gut* things take time to grow," Ella Mae said softly. "Maybe don't take it too seriously, this first date . . . chust see what happens? And keep your heart open to see what *Gott* might have in mind for ya."

Liz nodded. *I must remember that.*

The sun cast long shadows across the tree-lined section of road as Liz headed toward home. She noticed the spot where she'd offered Ashley Hyatt a ride earlier and hoped that, in due time, the Hyatts' neighbors and the People in general might accept, if not befriend, the family. "*Gut things take time to grow,*" Ella Mae had said about Matt. Didn't the same thing apply to relationships with the owners of the Christmas House?

At home, Mamm was warming up leftovers. "It'll just be the two of us for supper," she announced. "Martha Rose will be havin' the evening meal with her beau and his family before Singing."

"She'll enjoy that." Liz put two plates on the table and poured cold water from the fridge into two tumblers. "I had tea with Ella Mae this afternoon."

"I imagine she was happy for the company."

Liz sighed, then told her that Matt had asked her out. "Monday's an odd day for a date, but he lives too far away to come with his horse and buggy on a Saturday or Sunday. So he's sendin' a driver to pick me up tomorrow afternoon."

Mamm didn't show any sign of surprise. "Sounds like he's thought of everything, ain't so?"

Right then, Martha Rose came downstairs all dressed up for her supper date, her blond hair perfectly parted down the middle and her crisp white *Kapp* set just so on her head.

Liz smiled. "You look nice."

"I'll see ya at Singing," Martha replied.

"Thought I'd stay home tonight, actually."

"Not sick, I hope."

"*Nee*, just spendin' time with Mamm, and I need to start addressing my Christmas cards."

"Well, I'll miss singin' with ya, sister."

Mamm gave Martha Rose a gentle hug. "You enjoy yourself, dear."

Seeing the glow on her sister's face gave Liz some measure of hope about tomorrow. But she couldn't help wondering if she'd feel comfortable around Matt, despite what Ella Mae had said.

What if the date doesn't go well? Will that make things awkward for Matt and me on the buggy tours?

During supper, Mamm mentioned that Dat had indicated in his latest letter that he planned to arrive home early Christmas Eve afternoon. "Lord willin'."

"Just in time for Christmas Day," Liz said.

Mamm nodded, eyes bright. "I best be doin' some shoppin'."

Liz was delighted to see Mamm elated with anticipation.

All will be well.

14

Bill, the driver, pulled into her lane right on time, and Liz wasn't surprised to see the passenger van nearly full of Amishwomen heading out for an afternoon of shopping.

Once again, the day was fair with abundant sunshine and no sign of clouds. A mile or so up the road, Liz noticed the neighbors' steers had been turned out into stubby cornfields. Farther on, toward Intercourse Village, she saw large Christmas wreaths on shops and hotels and on the lampposts past the intersection of Route 340 and Ronks Road. And there were inflatable snowmen and Santas displayed in the yards of several homes, as well.

When they arrived at the Bird-in-Hand Bakery and Cafe, Matt was waiting for her near the entrance. The shyness she'd experienced when he'd asked her out rose up once more, but she recalled how peaceful she'd felt at Ella Mae's yesterday and took a deep breath. She was determined to get to know Matt better without putting any expectations on either of them.

Matt smiled when he saw her and walked toward her. "I'm

glad you're here," he said, and she noticed he'd dressed like he was going to church, just as he had that first day working for her.

She, too, had worn her best blue dress, cape, and matching apron. "Nice to see ya, too," she said.

Inside the bakery and cafe, they stood at the counter and looked over the dessert options on the menu board overhead, bedecked with silvery garland. Liz chose a serving of apple dumplings and Matt a slice of shoofly pie.

A few minutes later, a busload of tourists arrived, and people began lining up right behind them. "What timing," Matt whispered to her.

Liz agreed, still feeling oddly like she was out with someone she hardly knew. It wasn't that Matt's demeanor was any different—perhaps it was just the setting. *No distractions from tour customers or preparations to make for the workday.*

"Would ya like to sit upstairs where it's quieter?" Matt asked when their orders were ready and they'd gotten their coffees.

"Okay." Liz headed for the stairs with him, wondering if he'd thought through every aspect of their date.

They found a small table near the sliding glass door that led to an outside deck with a view of the farmers market across the road. Once they were seated, Matt said, "Let's ask the blessing," and they bowed their heads for the usual silent prayer.

Afterward, Liz reached for her coffee and took a sip. *It's just a casual date, Lord. Help me relax*, she prayed silently.

Matt asked about her Sunday.

She thought of the lovely tea with Ella Mae, and before that, the sermon at Preaching service. "Your Dat's cousin Preacher Yoder gave the first sermon," she told him. "And later, I ran into Ashley Hyatt on the road." She paused. "Well, I didn't actually hit her."

"*Des gut.*" Matt chuckled.

"I gave her a ride home, and she told me why their family moved to the hollow."

Matt's eyes widened, and he left his shoofly pie untouched as she told how the Hyatts had left behind a big city in favor of life on a small acreage. "Logan evidently had some farmin' experience," Liz added.

"*Jah*, he did mention to me 'bout helping on his uncle's farm as a boy. He liked the idea of havin' a big vegetable garden of his own." Matt forked into his slice of pie at last. "They plan to rent out the larger portion of their land at some point."

"Well, if they rent to an Amish farmer, that might help smooth over some of the tension in the hollow," she replied, then took another bite of her delicious apple dumpling, a perfect blend of tart and sweet.

"Was it Ashley's first time in a buggy?" Matt asked.

"I think so. She looked tired from her run but seemed glad to have someone to talk to." Liz didn't go into everything Ashley had shared with her. "Ever since, I've been tryin' to think of somethin' I could do to help them get more connected in the neighborhood."

"I can see why." He paused, studying her. "S'pose you're prayin' for wisdom 'bout that."

Liz nodded. "Prayer always helps, for certain." After they finished their desserts, another Amish couple came upstairs and sat across the room from them. They talked so pleasingly to each other in *Deitsch*, exchanging smiles as they ate their chocolate cake. Liz noticed the beginnings of a beard on the young man, indicating they were newlyweds.

Matt glanced at them and waved. "How 'bout that. That's my cousin and his wife . . . married last month."

"They're a little older than some couples," she observed softly.

Matt smiled. "Like us."

Her heart skipped a beat at his reply. *He thinks we're a couple?*

Matt leaned forward at the table, his gaze intent on her. He lowered his voice. "I know ya might wonder why I haven't settled down yet. I was seein' a girl for quite some time." He looked down at the crumbs on his plate for a moment. "Arie passed away unexpectedly from cancer two years ago—gone less than three months after her diagnosis."

"I am so sorry," Liz managed to say. "I had no idea, Matt."

He gazed out the sliding door, quiet for a long moment. "I'll be honest, it set me back for the longest time."

She searched his face. Her heart ached for him. "Of course it would. What a terrible loss."

He nodded ever so slowly, eyes solemn, and she wondered if he would say more.

"Eventually, though, I forced myself to be around people again, made myself go to Singings and whatnot."

She nodded, hanging on every word.

"I started helpin' with setting up the benches for house church, extra things like that." He leaned back in his chair.

"Maybe you're wonderin' why *I'm* still single," she ventured, reaching again for her coffee mug.

He smiled and nodded. "Your Dat did say you were when he contacted me 'bout helpin' ya. He didn't say much else, though."

Liz blushed at the idea of Dat trying to set her up, then felt it was time to mention Calvin Kinsinger. "After my last beau and I dated a while, we both seemed to know we weren't meant for each other. That was a year ago, and he's moved away since. It wasn't a hard loss like yours, though."

Matt smiled again. "I'm glad ya shared that, Liz." He paused, looking into her soul, it seemed. "And that ya trusted me . . . just one of the many things I appreciate 'bout you."

She felt something rise in her as their eyes met and held. Her face warmed at his compliment. "*Denki.* I appreciate you, too."

15

The air was nippy and damp early the next morning as Liz made her way out to the stable to groom King. Gently, she spoke to him while making circular motions with the curry comb, recalling that Matt liked to talk to the horse, too. "It'll be nice to see Matt again, won't it?"

As if he understood, the horse whinnied.

She laughed softly. "Well, Matt's fond of you, too."

The memory of her first date with him continued to linger. *It went very well*, she thought, *once I let myself enjoy it and not be worried about what comes next. Like Ella Mae said.*

She sighed deeply, thinking of the heartbreaking loss Matt had suffered. *I'm not sure I could let myself love again if that happened to me.*

Despite Liz's growing attraction to Matt, they continued to interact professionally and effectively with each other that work week. But when they groomed King together after the last ride of the day—a routine now—she was surprised at how easy it was to banter with him and even flirt a little. She no longer wondered what was happening between them. She absolutely knew.

Liz was happy to see the Nolt family return for the Christmas House Buggy Tour that Saturday afternoon, along with other customers. Jack and James, the identical twins, asked their parents if they could sit close to the front of the carriage. Their shy sister, Danica, sat with their parents, farther back.

"We're ready for the Christmas treats," Jack told Liz before the tour even started.

Liz smiled as James gave an emphatic nod. She recalled their question last month about the goodies on this particular tour.

"It'll be worth the wait, I can tell ya."

Jack made a show of rubbing his little hands together.

"Did I hear ya say you're just here for the treats?" Matt joked, getting into the driver's seat. Now that Matt knew all the routes for the tours, Liz had relinquished the reins more than a week ago. She liked having more freedom to interact with the passengers.

"Not *just* for the treats, the toy store, too," James said, elbowing his twin.

Danica looked downright embarrassed back there next to her mother as they headed out, driving past several farms and meadows on the way to the first stop at the Amish Toy Store. Liz enjoyed seeing the boys wave at two sorrel horses with long noses leaning over a fence as if watching the carriage go by. *Do I take these everyday scenes for granted?* she wondered. *There's so much to love about life here.*

The toy store was as popular as any stop, and the owner's young wife welcomed them and offered a quick peek through the window at the large woodworking shop in the back. Afterward, tourists were always eager to see the toy options on the store's shelves.

Liz noticed the Nolt twins eyeing wooden bulldozers, fire trucks, and a helicopter. Their father leaned down to ask each of them to choose one for a Christmas present, and their mother said she would wrap them for under the tree. The boys' eyes danced with excitement, yet their sister hung back. *Like she did at the petting zoo farm*, Liz remembered.

Going over to her, she asked, "Have ya seen the doll-sized rocking chairs? There's a dollhouse, too."

Instantly, Danica brightened.

"*Kumme*, I'll show ya." Liz led the way, and Danica's mom fell in step with them.

Later, once all the purchases were made, the touring carriage resumed its horse-drawn journey down Hickory Lane, then over toward the narrow road where the Christmas House was located. As they drew closer to the big display, Liz could hear the usual raucous music and saw two frowning Amishmen standing out near the road, arms folded as they observed.

In front of the Christmas House, Matt brought King to a halt so everyone could see the multitude of decorations and lights. Jack and James began to sway to the rhythmic beat.

"I can't believe the work they put into this," Patricia said.

"It's so creative," another passenger agreed.

Unexpectedly, five Amish schoolchildren on individual kick scooters—each child wearing a safety vest—zoomed past the horse and carriage, then stopped and stared in wonder at the dazzling lights.

On board the carriage, people stretched their necks to get a better glimpse of the adorable children—little girls in black coats and black outer bonnets, and the boys all in black from their knit hats and scarves down to their shoes.

This isn't a school day, Liz thought, curious why they'd come.

One woman held up her phone to take a photo, and Matt

politely asked her to respect the Amish wish that they not be photographed. Liz exchanged glances with Matt, proud of him for speaking up.

Suddenly, the door of the Christmas House opened, and a white miniature poodle dashed down the front steps, yipping and wagging its tail, and headed straight toward the scooters.

Ashley and her younger son, Jace, followed a second later and ran after the dog, calling, "Here, Kippy Sue. Come back, girl!" Yet the more they called and pleaded, the faster the little poodle ran from them, heading up the country road.

Immediately, the Amish children took off on their scooters, chasing after Kippy and calling to her in *Deitsch*. The tour passengers stood to watch, and it wasn't long before Ashley and her son vanished from sight, as well.

Never had Liz seen such a commotion during her tours here, and she wished she, too, could take time to help catch the Hyatts' small pooch, especially what with all the traffic soon to come, but she asked everyone to please be seated. "We need to be safe when we move forward to better view the nativity and angel chorus on the other side of the yard."

Cody Nolt spoke up. "Isn't it unusual for Amish children to show an interest in a Christmas display like this?"

"It's the first time I've seen any Amish children here," Liz replied. "And the first time for a dog chase durin' a tour, too."

Now that things had quieted down outside the carriage, she could hear the music for the display of Santa's sprightly elves, and the figures began to shift into another round of their dance.

Matt asked, "Who'd like to sing along?"

In the second row of the carriage, Jack and James began to sing "Jingle Bells" with Matt, and soon the others joined in, too. Danica had little bells on the wrists of her Christmas sweater, and she began to ring them in time to the song.

Liz stole an admiring glance at Matt again, trying to be subtle, but her heart beat faster. *He brings out the best in everyone!*

At Ella Mae's, Liz introduced her to the tour group standing there on the back porch. "Many thanks to my longtime friend for her tasty Christmas cookies and creamy hot cocoa. Ella Mae certainly helps spread Christmas cheer, *jah?*"

The group applauded, happy for the goodies, including gingerbread cookies and sand tarts topped with colorful sprinkles. The twins walked over to hand Ella Mae a tip like others had done on previous tours, thanking her for "the best cookies ever," which made Ella Mae smile, her dear face simply beaming.

"Have yourselves a nice time," Ella Mae told the boys as she leaned on her cane. "*En hallicher Grischtdaag*—a Merry Christmas to all of yous!"

Liz could well guess where that tip money would go—directly into the deacon's alms fund.

The ride back through Hickory Hollow was a jovial one as Cody Nolt got everyone singing carols, his strong baritone voice leading out. Liz couldn't resist joining in to sing "We Wish You a Merry Christmas."

As they waited to make the left-hand turn onto Cattail Road, Liz could see the long line of cars to the left inching toward the intersection, undoubtedly heading for the Christmas House. She wondered how the touring carriage would ever get across and hoped that Ashley and Jace and their dog were safely home.

Several cars farther back blared their horns, impatient with the wait, and everyone on board stopped their singing. There was no sign of the traffic letting up, however. Cars kept drifting through the intersection, blocking it completely, as though King and the carriage were invisible.

At last, Matt asked Liz to take the reins, and she scooted over to the right side of the carriage. Matt got out, reached for a flashlight in the glove compartment, and strode calmly into the clogged road, raising his right hand to stop the very next car while motioning with his left for Liz to direct King forward.

Liz held her breath, hoping the horse wouldn't be spooked as she carefully guided him through the narrow opening.

"Keep goin'," Matt called to her as she passed by. "I'll meet ya later."

Liz nodded, concerned he wouldn't be so visible soon, now that the sun was setting. *Lord, please protect him*, she prayed silently as she guided King back toward the parking lot of the hardware store, astonished at the number of cars coming from Route 340. The northbound lane was vacant of vehicles, so the traffic heading south had to be there primarily for the Christmas House.

The image of Matt courageously taking charge and standing in the road, nearly sandwiched between the cars, made her shiver inwardly. Even so, her only responsibility now was to her passengers, and she steadily held the driving lines until she got them back safely.

She'd nearly finished grooming King by the time Matt came walking across the parking lot. Her first impulse was to run to greet him, but she resisted.

"You'll never guess what happened," he said as he approached. "The Hyatts' dog reappeared, runnin' *holler-boller* amongst the cars. The poor thing came right up to me, it was so frightened. I was able to catch her."

"Aww, *wunnerbaar.*" She shook her head, grateful Kippy Sue's dangerous escape had come to an end.

"I must say, that was one happy family when they saw me with the pup."

"You are so kind, Matt," said Liz, though other, more endearing words came to mind.

16

The expected snow and colder weather finally arrived in mid-December, as if Old Man Winter had turned the switch. On Thursday, Liz received something in the mail from Matt and smiled all the way up the driveway and into the house. In her room, she opened the envelope and found a lovely Christmas card and a handwritten note: *Dear Liz, my sweet friend, I'd like to take you out for supper sometime before Christmas. We can discuss it this Saturday before or after the riding tours, if you'd like. I'm looking forward to spending time with you again! Matt Yoder*

Smiling, she set the card on her dresser. Then, going over to the farm calendar hanging on her closet door, she looked at all the local events coming up: ice skating tomorrow afternoon, caroling on Saturday evening, the Amish school Christmas play next Friday, and on the next Saturday evening, *Die Youngie* were having their annual Christmas Eve supper. The next day would be Christmas.

Ach, how will I fit everything in? she wondered, not accustomed to having such a wonderful predicament.

After the noon meal and visits from their regular egg customers, Liz and Martha Rose went shopping to purchase presents for both Mamm and Dat. Her sister had already shopped with Cousin Fran to buy gifts for other family members, including Liz.

Their driver let them out at the Old Candle Barn in Intercourse Village and agreed to return in one hour. The place was well-decorated for Christmas with wreaths of all kinds and candles galore, some scented in floral fragrances and others unscented, such as tapers or even chunky pillar candles.

"Did ya bring a list?" Martha Rose asked.

Liz tapped her forehead. "It's all up here."

"Anything for Matt, just maybe?" Martha probed.

"I doubt we're exchangin' gifts."

Martha smirked. "Don't be silly."

"We're here for Mamm and Dat," Liz reminded her.

Martha nodded reluctantly, like she'd rather talk about Matt. "I'm thinkin' Mamm needs a new cutting board."

Since they were in no rush, they strolled through all the aisles just for fun—the tinware and pottery, then the dry goods, and took their time looking at the braided rugs, too. With all the potpourri and whatnot, the former barn smelled just glorious.

"Surely they have cutting boards," Liz said, looking around.

"We'll find them. Let's keep goin'."

Liz kept pace with her sister. "Last time I was here, I told Mamm you could get lost in this store."

"No kiddin'."

In their search, Liz spotted some beautiful oil lamps. "I think Dat would like one of these."

Martha tilted her head as if imagining where he might put it. "*Jah*, it would go nicely near his reading chair upstairs."

Liz found the tall one in a box below the display and carried it carefully.

Eventually, they located a display of cutting boards and chose a good, solid one that was affordable. Since Martha was only given a monthly allowance from the egg sales, Liz planned to pay the majority of the price.

Liz carried the oil lamp and Martha Rose took the cutting board to the register up front.

"You girls found some real nice things," the woman cashier remarked cheerfully, offering each of them a small candy cane from a red ceramic cup on the counter.

"We sure enjoyed browsing," Martha Rose told her. "Your store's always so perty, but 'specially at Christmastime."

The cashier smiled. "But nothing quite as done up as the Christmas House down in Hickory Hollow. Have you seen it?"

"Have we?" Martha Rose laughed. "We live less than a mile from it."

"Is that right?"

Liz nodded. "How'd ya hear 'bout it?"

"There was a short segment on the local news last evening," the woman said.

"On television?" Martha's eyebrows rose.

Liz groaned inwardly. *Now there'll be even more traffic and complaints from Amish neighbors.*

Liz woke up to a brilliant landscape. Gazing down at the pastureland, she could see where the snow had drifted during the windy night. The sky was clearing now, and the tree branches near the house were ever so still beneath the fresh layer of white.

She dressed, then helped make omelets for breakfast and afterward swept the kitchen floor. Meanwhile, Mamm and Martha Rose washed dishes and decided what kind of cookies to make for the annual cookie exchange tomorrow afternoon, which Liz would miss due to her Saturday tours. And tomorrow night was caroling with *die Youngie*, too, but if Matt wanted to stay and talk after work, she would rather stick around for that.

"Be sure to make some gingerbread men, and maybe little gingerbread houses, too," Liz suggested, remembering what a big hit Ella Mae's cookies had been with the children on the recent tours.

"Do we even have a house-shaped cookie cutter?" Martha asked, looking puzzled.

"Didn't Gracie give Mamm one along with several others last year for Christmas?" Liz replied.

"*Ach*, forgot 'bout that." Martha Rose went to look in the small pantry at the opposite end of the kitchen.

A short while later, Liz saw Onkel Joe out in the driveway with his horse-drawn plow. "Joe said he'd be lookin' out for us while Dat and Adam are gone."

"Awful nice of him," Mamm said, going to the window with Liz and peering out.

The snow looked to be about half a foot deep. *A good day to stay in and finish the knit scarf*, Liz thought, knowing now who she'd be giving it to.

While the dozens of cookies were cooling, Mamm worked on making more hand muffs for Liz to sell, and Martha strung up the Christmas cards that had arrived in the mail today, adding them to the others already hanging in the doorway between the sitting room and front room.

"Now we just need some paper snowflakes for the windows," Martha Rose said.

"But you'll cover up the frosty designs." Liz laughed.

Mamm nodded. "*Jah*, let's leave the Good Lord's handiwork for now."

Later, Liz went ice skating with Martha Rose and a group of

their girl cousins, including Fran and Naomi. Secretly, Liz wished Matt could have been there, but she made the best of it, looking forward very much to seeing him tomorrow at work.

On Saturday, a week before Christmas Eve, Liz brought out the sleigh from the carriage shed with help from Reuben and Henry, who were there to muck out the horse and mule stalls. Her brothers quickly hitched King to the open sleigh, and Liz was glad she'd bundled up, even though the temperatures were to be less wintry than yesterday. All the same, Mamm gave her plenty of hand muffs in case some of today's passengers hadn't worn mittens, and Liz had enough heavy woolen lap blankets for everyone. *Although it's chilly, the open sleigh will make the experience more festive and exciting.*

On the way to the hardware store parking lot, she saw Bishop John Beiler out hitching his road horse to the family carriage. He waved and she waved back. *Does he know about the Christmas House being on television?*

She planned to tell Matt first thing when she saw him. Just knowing she'd be spending the day with him again, her heart fluttered. "Oh goodness," she murmured, her breath hanging in the air. "He seems like everything I've been waitin' for."

As it turned out, Matt told *her* about the TV segment when she arrived. "Word's spreadin' 'bout the decked-out farmhouse in the middle of Amish farmland," Matt told her. "So we need to find a different way to get back here after the cookie stop at Ella Mae's."

"It'll take a little longer, but you're right."

"Can't risk spookin' King again in all that traffic." Matt rubbed the horse's long neck.

Liz opened her shoulder bag and gave him her Christmas card. "I received your perty one, Matt. And the nice note, too. *Denki.*"

He thanked her and placed the card in his black coat pocket.

"And to answer your invitation," she said, "I could have supper with ya December 23 if that'll work."

"Perfect! I'll ride over with my favorite driver this time. That way we can be together longer." He winked at her, his face aglow.

Her own face suddenly felt warm, and she wondered if he noticed. "That'll be real nice."

17

While Liz, Mamm, and Martha Rose were visiting Henry and his wife, Ida, and their family on Sunday afternoon, Mamm got to talking about how much fun the Sisters Day gathering had been last month and let it slip that her daughter-in-law Gracie had urged her the Saturday before to "wear your for-good clothes."

Martha Rose grinned as they sat at Ida's kitchen table enjoying lemon meringue pie. "Liz an' I figured somethin' was up when we noticed that."

"Well, to Gracie's credit," Mamm said, "she didn't actually say what was goin' to happen. Just for me to look nice."

"That was *gut* of her," Liz said, laughing.

"Well, it was downright peculiar that Gracie would just come over to pick me up Saturday morning, unplanned," Mamm said with a glance at Liz. "Wasn't born yesterday, ya know."

Liz and Martha Rose covered their mouths in amusement.

Snow was falling on Friday afternoon, two days before Christmas, as Liz, Mamm, and Martha Rose stepped into the family buggy to head for the Christmas program at the schoolhouse on Cattail Road. Liz loved going to the nativity play every year, but she was especially happy this year because some of her older cousins' children would be playing a part, as well as Reuben's daughter Mary Ruth.

When Mamm directed the horse to the shoulder to park on the road near the schoolhouse, Liz could see small groups of men talking here and there in the schoolyard.

"Looks like they're chewin' the fat 'bout something," Mamm said, setting the parking brake.

Liz didn't have to wonder what. The way heads were wagging and hands flapping, she was almost certain they were having their say about all the traffic bringing outsiders from all over to see the Christmas House.

As Liz tied the horse to the fence post, she heard one of the men, voice raised, saying, "I couldn't get home from the smithy's last night for the longest time, the road was so crammed with cars. Same thing happened to my neighbors."

Another farmer spoke up. "My sinful nature's tempted me to go over and unplug that there music and all the Christmas lights. Ain't jokin', neither."

A third man agreed. "*Jah*, at this point, I can scarcely wait for Christmas to be over and done with."

Hearing this made Liz sad, yet she understood firsthand how challenging it could be to manage driving on the main road leading into the hollow come late afternoon.

This time of year should be joyful . . . not like this, she thought as she stepped in line to enter the schoolhouse with Mamm and Martha Rose when the bell began to toll.

During the nativity play, Liz spotted her young school-age cousins—four shepherds and one small lamb who forgot to remain on all fours and simply sat down at one point. This brought a wave of hushed laughter from the audience.

Liz's taller cousins were angels, and surprisingly, Reuben's daughter, who was not exactly angelic by nature, played the part quite convincingly when the manger tipped suddenly and the lifelike doll representing Jesus was at risk of falling out. Thanks to her quick actions, the babe in the manger was spared.

"A little added drama," Martha Rose whispered to Liz, who had to squelch her laugh.

By the end of the play and after the traditional presentation of gifts to the schoolteacher, the snow had slowed some, though the forecast was for more to come. On the ride home next to Mamm in the driver's seat, Martha Rose recounted all the afternoon's humorous unscripted events. But it was Mamm who brought up the consensus of the People, having heard from a good many womenfolk that they disliked the Santa Claus on the Hyatts' roof and all the secular parts of the display. "If they had to make a show of things, why not just play up the manger scene?"

Liz agreed but listened carefully as Mamm continued.

"They and their husbands actually regret Logan Hyatt and his family movin' to Hickory Hollow."

Liz felt sorry that everyone was seemingly against the Hyatts, recalling Ashley Hyatt's remark that they still felt a bit lonely.

What can be done? Liz wondered even after returning home and beginning to prepare for her supper date with Matt.

Snow began to fall thicker that evening, and by the time Matt's driver, Bill Kline, pulled up close to the back door, Liz wondered if she ought to take along her snow boots. But Matt was already out of the van, waving and smiling and sliding the back passenger door open.

"It's really makin' down," she said as she pulled on her knitted mittens and stepped outside.

"Perfect for a pre-Christmas supper." He helped her into the van.

They sat together on the second bench seat. Two other passengers were seated behind them, both Amishwomen whom Liz didn't recognize, but she greeted them all the same.

"Can ya guess where we're goin'?" Matt asked her quietly.

"Give me a hint."

"Let's see, there's a large selection of food." He smiled at her.

"Well, there'd have to be." She laughed softly, trying to think where he'd want to take her that wasn't too busy so close to Christmas. "How about a real hint?" she said.

"It has a fireplace in the large dining room."

Most of the nicer local restaurants had fireplaces, though. She thought for a while, then gave up. "I can't guess."

"Then you'll just have to wait an' see," he said, gently bumping his shoulder against hers.

Liz thrilled to his attention. "I'll try to be patient," she replied, wondering if the women behind them were observing Matt's rather affectionate manner.

Bill stopped the van in front of the restaurant at the Hershey Farm Resort, which had been completely rebuilt since a fire destroyed both the restaurant and the gift shop. Matt told Bill when to return for them, then, getting out of the van, he offered his hand to help Liz walk down a shoveled pathway to the entrance. It was a good thing, too, since the fresh snow would have come up higher than her for-good shoes.

Inside, the interior was beautiful and welcoming and decorated for the holidays. It was obvious they'd arrived ahead of the supper crowd since the greeter immediately led them to a quiet table near the fireplace, which had its mantel adorned with spruce boughs laced with tiny white lights. A string of brass bells cascaded down each side. On the table, a tall green taper was already lit, accentuating the white linen tablecloth. Liz was glad she'd worn her best clothing despite the snowstorm, wanting to look extra nice for Matt.

Soon, the waiter came to take their orders, and both of them chose the golden fried chicken with mashed potatoes and gravy instead of the all-you-can-eat buffet, although Liz requested buttered carrots for her vegetable and Matt selected the squash medley.

When they were alone, Matt looked at her admiringly. "It's nice we could see each other like this before Christmas," he said. "And . . . before our last tour together."

Liz hadn't wanted to think about that, but tomorrow *was* Christmas Eve, after all, and her brother and father were due to return from Somerset. *Adam will expect to resume working with me after Christmas*, she thought sadly.

Without warning, tears sprang to her eyes.

Fortunately, the waiter came to pour ice water into their goblets at just that moment, and she was able to quickly blink her tears away and lower her gaze, looking at the lovely place setting.

"You okay, Liz?" he asked after the waiter left.

She inhaled, trying to gain the upper hand with her emotions—her tears had surprised her. "Such a perty place here, ain't so?"

He glanced around. "They've done a great job rebuilding it. Many Amish worked on it; I know that much."

"Did you help, too?"

"Only for a week or so before I was called away to smaller jobs in houses and whatnot."

She had to wonder if he missed doing his construction and repair work, but she didn't want to bring that up just now. Not while feeling this tenderhearted about not seeing him much after tomorrow.

"Listen, Liz, I'd like to stay in touch with you." He smiled so sweetly, she could almost guess what he was going to say. "I enjoy your company . . . I hope to see ya again after the holidays."

"I'd like that, too," she admitted. *He's not asking to court*, she thought as their salads were served.

Matt reminisced about some of the highlights of the tours they'd experienced together. Watching his expression as she listened to the warm way he talked about the people they'd met, she realized just how much she would miss having him along.

Adam just doesn't have the same way with folks.

After dessert, they lingered. *Matt's not in a hurry, either*, she thought, *even with the snow surely stacking up.* She was thankful they had this quiet moment together before the busy days of Christmas Eve and Christmas arrived, and then Second Christmas the next day, with more relatives coming for dinner—extended family they couldn't accommodate all at once around Mamm's table.

It was only when they were waiting in the restaurant's lobby for the driver that she noticed how very deep the snow had become. "I wonder if people will want to risk comin' out in this weather tomorrow for the tours," she said.

Matt shook his head. "They'll likely cancel if this keeps up."

She thought of giving her cousin Roy a quick call while they were near a telephone, just to check if there had been any cancellations via the website, but Bill pulled up just then.

The wind picked up and swirled the snow along the freshly shoveled path to the van. Inside, Matt suggested they sit in the far back to make it convenient for other possible passengers to climb in. Liz wondered, too, if it was so they could have a little more privacy this time.

It was slow going even with few cars on the road, the visibility less than a quarter mile or so. Snow was falling sideways, and she wondered how bad this storm would get as Matt and Bill discussed the inclement weather.

"The heaviest snowfall is heading straight for Hickory Hollow," Bill said.

We should've left sooner, Liz thought, but Matt didn't seem concerned.

Bill turned the radio to some Christmas music, and Liz stared out the window at the twirling snow. From time to time, she could feel the gusts of wind shake the van. "O Holy Night" came on just then, and she prayed silently for their safety.

A few minutes later, Bill's phone rang, and Liz heard him say, "I'll certainly do that. Thanks, and you too."

The brief conversation ended, and Bill looked into his rearview mirror. "That was your cousin Roy, Liz. I'd mentioned to him when I ran into him earlier today that you'd be riding with me this evening, and he wanted to be sure to catch you, letting you know that your tour reservations for tomorrow have all been cancelled due to the snowstorm. He also left a voicemail on your father's barn phone."

"*Denki*," Liz said, relieved. "*Gut* to know."

Another gust of wind swayed the van, and Liz inhaled sharply.

Matt reached for her hand and held it. "You're all right," he said softly. "Bill will be sure to get you safely home, Lizzy."

Hearing him call her that caught her off-guard. Only close relatives referred to her by the nickname. But being with him like this, her hand nestled now in both of his, was a warm comfort in the midst of this awful blizzard.

18

The snow continued as they drove east, nearly blinding at times. Liz wondered how Bill could see well enough to navigate the typically busy highway. Occasionally, Liz could make out the glow of lights from a hotel or shops, but as the snow thickened, the highway became lost in the unbroken storm. It was unsettling to her, and she felt dizzy as she stared out the window.

Eventually, Bill made the turn north onto Hershey Church Road, then Cattail Road, and Liz peered out the window again, trying to make out the familiar landmarks, including the bishop's big farm on the left that now literally blended into the whiteness. She was stunned at how different everything looked with all the snow piling up. Dat had once called a storm like this a whiteout, she recalled.

As they headed onward, Matt sat up straight, as if trying to see the road ahead. The sky seemed to have lowered, limiting the visibility even more, and she realized she was gritting her teeth as they passed the general store with its nearly flat roof and the hitching posts along its front cloaked in white.

When they turned onto the road that led past the Christmas

House with only the van's headlights to guide the way, Liz could scarcely make out the shape of the farmhouses she knew were scattered here and there. The snow masked trees, horse fences, and outbuildings. Even Logan Hyatt's renowned display was difficult to spot in the tempest. And as they moved slowly along, it dawned on Liz. "Look!" she said to Matt. "All the Christmas lights are off . . . and the house is dark, too."

"If they're without electric, it could be a problem," Matt said.

"Well, a while back, I noticed a small stack of chopped wood behind the house," Bill said, glancing up at the roof. "There *is* a chimney, so they must at least have a wood-burning stove or fireplace."

After mentioning the work he had done there, Matt confirmed they did, in fact, have a wood-burning stove, but only in the front room. Hearing this was a slight comfort to Liz, but seeing the Christmas trappings nearly buried in snow seemed so very strange. Gone were the alluring lights and merry music that had disturbed so many neighbors.

"Folks nearby will have a quieter night," Matt whispered to her.

Liz was silent, pondering all of this and hoping the Hyatt family would have enough warmth for the time being.

A short distance past the Christmas House, the snow on the road became so deep that the underside of the van scraped the drifts. Bill slowed to a stop and put the van's gear in reverse, attempting to back up. He shifted the gears again, and the wheels began to spin. Again and again, he tried to back up, to get free of the snowdrift.

"I'm afraid we're stuck," he said at last, putting on the emergency blinkers. He used his phone to call for assistance, but after the call ended, he turned in his seat to tell them that it would be an hour or more before help arrived. "Sounds like all of Hickory Hollow and a large swath of Salisbury Township to the east are without power due to downed power lines. And it likely won't be restored for at least a couple days."

Matt glanced at Liz with a concerned look, then at Bill. "I'd hate to leave ya here, but maybe Liz an' I should just walk the rest of the way."

"Only if you think you can make it all right." Bill sounded hesitant. "It's always best to stay in the vehicle during such a storm, even without heat."

"My house is only one farm away," Liz said, trying to sound braver than she felt. "Not that far." Then quietly, she told Matt, "You can stay at our place, if need be." *Mamm wouldn't mind*, she thought.

"It won't seem like a short jaunt in this storm," Bill warned.

There was a pause, the wailing wind the only sound except for the snow against the windows.

"The longer we wait," Liz urged, "the worse it could get." She shivered at the thought.

The atmosphere in the vehicle was solemn, and Liz didn't want to be the one making the final decision, no matter how badly she wanted to get home. *What would Dat and Mamm say to do?*

"Do ya have a blanket or something Liz could wrap up in, maybe?" Matt asked at last.

Bill pointed toward the very back of the van. "There's a waterproof tarp behind the seat where you're sitting."

Matt reached over the back of the seat to get the lightweight folded tarp. "We'll be very careful, and I'll watch over Liz. Oh, and would ya mind leavin' a message on my Dat's barn phone, so my folks know where I'll be tonight?"

"I'll do that," Bill said. "I have their number." He paused, then added, "When you can, Matt, give me a call from the Lantzes' barn phone. I'll rest easier knowing you and Liz got there safely."

"I will," Matt promised. He removed his straw hat and took out a black knit hat from his coat pocket. "I'll have to leave my hat here in the van, if ya don't mind."

"I'll see that you get it back," Bill said.

Matt reached to open the sliding door, and Liz got up from her seat.

Outside, Matt stamped his feet to make a landing spot for her to step down, then held up the tarp to place it over her head. From there on, the drifting snow swallowed her feet, almost knee-high at times as she pushed one foot, then the other, forward with great effort. Oh, she wished she'd brought her snow boots—her legs and dress were immediately soaked.

Matt held on to her with their every step, and thanks to Bill's tarp, both of them were somewhat protected from the lashing snow.

Liz tried to think of things to be thankful for as they crept forward deliberately, one being that she was young and strong enough for such a trek.

Who would've thought I'd end up plodding through drifts of snow after such a nice supper date?

Meanwhile, Matt kept his strong arm around her, not letting her fall, though several times she almost did. "I'm mighty sorry 'bout this," he said, his voice indistinct in the howling wind.

"We should be home soon," she reassured him, but she really didn't know for sure, because it was difficult to make out familiar sights. "We're goin' in the right direction, anyway."

Matt was silent for the longest time, and she hoped he wasn't regretting their decision to leave the van.

She squinted into the wind and asked God to help them find their way before either of them suffered frostbite.

Matt led her toward a section of the road where the snow was a little less deep, and they could walk more easily. She wouldn't tell him, but her feet and legs were numb, and her wet mittens were useless to keep her fingers warm.

The only other time she'd been out in a snowstorm like this, she and her brother Henry had taken the pony and cart over to the general store for Mamm. It had been years ago, and a sudden snow squall had come up when they were only halfway home. The difference between that storm and this one was that she and Henry had ridden in the cart during the daytime, and while the visibility was almost nil, the pony knew the way home.

I was only eight but unafraid since my older brother was with me, she recalled.

Thinking back to that long-ago day, Liz peered into the fury and thought she saw a candle in a window not far away. And as they walked onward, she could see even more candles shining in the upstairs and downstairs windows, little beacons in the night. Mamm's doing, she was sure. "That's my house," she told Matt, certain of it.

"A welcome sight." He sounded relieved.

"We're close now." She kept her eyes fixed on Mamm's battery-operated candles, and suddenly she had a wonderful-good idea.

"*Kumme en!* Yous are soaked to the skin," Mamm said as Liz and Matt clomped in the back door and removed the tarp. Her mother's face was pale, and she reached to touch Liz's cold cheek. "Oh, my dear . . ."

"The van got stuck in a drift—couldn't make it this far," Matt explained and asked if he could use the stable phone to let the driver know they'd made it here.

"*Ach*, I hate for ya to go back out in this." Mamm shook her head. "Can ya see your way out there?" She reached for a flashlight and gave it to him.

Matt took the flashlight and wet tarp and headed out the door again.

Martha Rose came into the utility room just then. "You're home," she said breathlessly. "I can't believe the driver let ya walk in this."

Liz explained that with Matt along, she'd felt safe. "But it was harder goin' than we expected. All that matters is we're home now."

"I'm so glad you're okay," Martha Rose said, eyes serious.

Mamm nodded and took Liz's wet coat and black outer bonnet to hang in the kitchen near the heater stove. "*Kumme* get warmed up, Lizzy."

She took off her wet shoes and stockings and left them in the utility room, then went to stand near the coal stove while Martha went to fetch blankets for them to wrap up in.

In a short time, Matt returned and joined Liz by the stove, barefoot. He placed his coat and knit hat near the stove on the floor and rubbed his hands together, his damp hair sticking up. "Bill was mighty relieved to hear from me. He'd already left a message for my Dat."

Liz was glad Matt's parents wouldn't worry.

"We began to pray when the snow started comin' so quick," Mamm said. "At least two inches an hour."

"I was prayin', too," Matt said quietly.

Liz looked up at him with respect. *He was worried but didn't let on.*

After a time, Mamm motioned for Matt to go with her. "Adam's room is clean and available," she said, heading through the kitchen to the other side of the sitting room.

"*Denki* for your hospitality," Matt said, and Liz could hear him as she and Martha Rose headed to the bathroom close to the kitchen, where she ran tepid water over her still-cold hands. "One of Mamm's muffs sure would've come in handy tonight."

"Can ya move your fingers?" Martha asked, a concerned frown on her face.

"*Jah.*" She began to move them, slowly at first. "'Tween you and me, I'm not sure how much farther we could've gone."

"Oh, sister, I kept wonderin' where you were . . . what was happenin'."

"The Lord was with us. I know that."

Liz heard Mamm telling Matt that he was welcome to wear anything he found in the closet or dresser drawers. "I 'spect you and Adam are close to the same size," she said.

Liz smiled, remembering how wary she'd been at just the thought of Matt taking Adam's spot with the tours, and here he was staying the night at her family's house.

After warming her hands with the lukewarm water, Liz patted them dry on the small towel. Then Martha Rose helped her remove the many straight pins from her wet cape and long apron before Liz patted herself with a bath towel, thinking how nice a warm bath or shower would be. But she wanted that for Matt, since he'd taken the brunt of the cold for her.

Liz told Martha about the power outage in Hickory Hollow and also farther to the east, thinking again of the Hyatts. "All the lights were off at the Christmas House, inside and out, even though it was all lit up when we passed by there earlier this evening." She also mentioned that the driver had been told about the many downed power lines when he called for roadside assistance. "Bill said the power would likely be out for a couple of days."

"We should pray for our English neighbors tonight," Martha Rose said.

"*Jah.*" Liz headed upstairs to her room and lit the gas lamp, got out of her damp clothes, and put on her warmest nightgown, thinking she would stay upstairs a while to give Matt his privacy since the downstairs bathroom was the only one in the house.

Sighing now as what they'd gone through began to sink in, she removed her hairpins and let down her damp hair. She still felt chilled, so she slipped on her long robe over her nightgown, got into bed, and pulled up her quilts, burrowing down like a gopher for the time being. She thanked God for helping her and Matt make it here safely.

Her breathing warmed the space beneath the covers, and she relived her special date with Matt and the challenge of getting home. And once again, she contemplated the idea forming in her heart.

I'll discuss it with Matt tomorrow.

19

In her dreams, Liz kept slogging through snow, stuck in the same spot. When she awakened and peeked under the shade and saw clear skies and sunshine, she was more than happy to put yesterday's struggles behind her.

She could hear someone shoveling outside as she dressed for the day, and after she'd put her hair up in its proper bun, she opened the shade and saw Matt and her brother Henry clearing the snow from the long walkway behind the house, Henry talking cordially with Matt as they worked.

At breakfast, Mamm asked Henry about the condition of the roads now, wondering aloud if Dat and Adam would be able to travel home from Somerset today as planned.

"It's possible the roads won't be drivable between here and Somerset," Henry suggested almost tentatively, as if regretting it. "The highways might be okay, but these back country roads will take some time to clear out, 'specially with power lines down."

"Onkel Joe has a small scraper plow," Martha Rose suggested hopefully.

Mamm nodded. "True, but he won't be able to do all the roads in the hollow," she said. "He has his own large property to plow, and he often does ours."

"And with this cold, who's to say how long before the snow will melt," Henry added, before excusing himself and heading out to do more shoveling.

There was a short lull as Mamm got up to pour more coffee for Matt. "A big horse like King could manage to get through the unplowed roads round here, ain't so?" Liz asked.

Mamm frowned. "Do you have something in mind?"

"We're all ears." Matt gave Liz a quick smile.

"I know the bishop's not too keen on us ridin' horses, but this is important." She began to share her brewing idea with the others.

When she finished explaining, Matt leaned forward, elbows on the table. "It's a great idea, Liz."

Martha Rose grinned as she looked back and forth between Matt and Liz, but Mamm's expression was anything but agreeable.

"There'll be no worry about being out and about now," Liz assured her softly, "what with the sun shinin' and the winds calm."

Matt nodded emphatically. "I'll go with ya, Liz. King can easily carry both of us."

At Matt's remark, Mamm's countenance altered, and after Liz borrowed some trousers from Adam's closet to wear under her long dress and apron, the two of them bundled up in their coats. This time, Liz wore her snow boots, and Matt wore Adam's.

Then, remembering the scarf and matching hat she'd knitted—and since it was Christmas Eve, after all—she removed her boots and hurried upstairs to get Matt's gift, unwrapped though it was.

When she returned, she gave them to him, and he promptly pulled on the knit hat and wrapped the scarf around his neck.

"Perfect timing," he said, winking at her. "A real nice gift. *Denki*, Liz."

She bent down and pulled on her snow boots yet again, feeling good about herself. "When I saw ya put on the knit hat last night, I wasn't sure ya'd need another one with a scarf to match."

His sweet smile and soft eyes seemed to indicate that if they'd been alone, he might've reached over to give her a grateful hug. But Mamm and Martha Rose were hovering near, so Matt's adoring expression was enough for now. "I'll get *gut* use out of these, for certain. *Denki* again."

"You're welcome," she said, delighted. "Now, let's get King out of the stable."

Thanks to Henry and Matt's earlier shoveling, they headed with ease down the walkway and up the driveway to the stable. "Glad ya like my idea," she told him.

And in the stable, where no one but the livestock could see, Matt reached for her and embraced her gently. She leaned her face against his big shoulder, warm down to her toes.

"This might just be the answer to your prayers," he whispered.

"I really hope so," she said, smiling as he released her and opened the door to King's stall. Matt placed the riding saddle on the big horse and led him out of the stable. Outside, he put his foot in the stirrup and hoisted himself into the saddle, then reached down with one arm to pull Liz up to sit behind him. With Liz holding tightly to Matt, they headed down the snowy driveway and turned right onto the snow-drifted road toward Onkel Joe's farm.

When they arrived, Liz got down from the horse and headed around to the back porch, where she encountered Joe coming down the steps. "*Gut* to see ya, Lizzy. What's up?" He waved at Matt, who nodded from his saddled perch.

"Power lines are down in the hollow," she began by saying,

then mentioned the Hyatts. "It's surely an inconvenience for them, if not a hardship. Could be a couple days."

"Didn't realize there's an outage," Onkel Joe said, reaching for the snow shovel propped against the porch banister.

"I have an idea to help the Hyatts 'til their electric is back on," she told him. "And what better time than at Christmas, *jah?*" She went on to ask if he could spare a quart jar of vegetables, some dried meats, or jams—and one battery-operated candle to donate to Logan Hyatt and his family. "If so—and if you can get there—meet me at the Christmas House this evening at seven-thirty. If each family does a little, together we can make a big difference."

"Well now, Lizzy." He gave her a quick smile. "This does sound like somethin' you'd think of."

"Will ya spread the word?"

"*Abselutt.*"

"This is just a start," she told him, following him down the walkway. "Matt an' I plan to stop by as many Amish farms in the hollow as possible."

"You're a kind young woman. *Gott* be with ya . . . and Matt, too." He bobbed his head toward Matt.

She hurried over to the horse and got back up. Holding on to Matt again, she told him how nice her uncle had been, and they made their way back toward the road. "Not even a speck of reluctance."

"*Des gut*, but be prepared to meet with resistance from most of the folks," Matt said over his shoulder. "It's unlikely everyone will be so agreeable, considerin' everything."

"I hope you're wrong." She held on more tightly as King began to trot.

Come what may, I believe God put this on my heart.

They spent the rest of the morning going from farmhouse to farmhouse, asking the People for a little neighborly help.

The day continued to be sunny but bitterly cold, and when Matt mentioned he'd like to try to make it home for Christmas Eve, Liz wholeheartedly agreed. Mamm insisted he wear Adam's snow boots and warmest coat to walk all the way out to the main crossroad to meet Bill. Liz went out and stood on the back porch with him, thanking him for going with her all over Hickory Hollow.

"Glad to help," he said. "We'll see what comes of it."

"Wouldn't ya like some hot cocoa before ya leave?" She hated to see him go.

"Another time, okay?"

She smiled and nodded.

"Have a real nice Christmas with your family, Lizzy."

She grinned at the nickname. "You too."

After he left, she got busy making pies for Christmas dinner tomorrow, since all her siblings and their families would come to celebrate the Lord's birthday with them. Martha Rose and Mamm had already cooked up a few of the side dishes this morning, and the other families were bringing the rest. Mamm and Liz would rise very early tomorrow morning, since the two large turkeys would require at least four hours to roast in the oven once they were stuffed. To get a head start, though, Mamm would mix together the dry ingredients for the dressing, keeping them separate from the wet ones, and refrigerate them overnight.

As always, Christmas dinner will be wonderful-good!

Once she had a free moment, Liz went out to the utility room to put on her coat and boots. She remembered being greeted so warmly by Mamm and Martha Rose yesterday when she and

Matt arrived from the blizzard. And there was the lovely memory of the unexpected though welcome hug from Matt in the stable this morning.

She walked down the driveway Onkel Joe had plowed while she and Matt were out going from house to house, curious to see if the mail had been delivered. A stretch of their country road had been cleared as well, and she assumed her thoughtful Onkel was responsible.

Opening the mailbox, she wasn't all that surprised to find nothing when she looked inside. Shivering and wondering where Dat and Adam might be—and praying they were all right—she hurried back toward the house.

Later that afternoon, Martha Rose told Liz, "I don't see how we'll get to Christmas Eve supper for the youth tonight. I mean, the girls won't want to ride horseback to get there, and the snow is too deep for a sleigh."

"Aww, then you won't get to see your beau," Liz replied.

Martha Rose pressed her lips together. "Honestly, I don't mind. I'd like to be here when Dat and Adam walk in that back door."

Studying her sister, Liz said thoughtfully, "A few of us will be over at the Christmas House by seven-thirty, if ya want to join us."

Not but a few minutes later, a knock came at the back door. Martha Rose hurried to answer it, and there was Ben Fisher, dressed for the cold weather in a black coat, knit hat, and a woolen scarf over his face. Only his eyes were showing.

"Just makin' the rounds to let everyone know there won't be a youth supper or caroling tonight as planned. We'll meet next Tuesday night for the postponed supper." His eyes crinkled as he smiled beneath the scarf. "Sorry," he said, lowering his voice. "I was lookin' forward to it and to goin' caroling with ya, too."

"Would ya like to come in and warm up?"

He brightened all the more. "I would, but I need to get the word out. Hope ya understand."

Martha Rose nodded. "Of course."

Ben smiled, turned slowly, and headed down the porch steps toward his saddled horse.

Liz, who'd overheard their conversation, waited for her sister to return to the kitchen. "You'll have tomorrow and Second Christmas to look forward to," she said, hoping that was of some comfort.

Martha's face was still aglow. "Well, this way, I can go with you and Mamm over to the Christmas House . . . if we can get there with the horse and buggy."

I wonder if any neighbors besides Onkel Joe will brave the weather to meet us there?

Before the sun set, Liz saddled up King, wanting to investigate the roads leading to the Christmas House prior to heading out later with Mamm and Martha Rose in the family buggy. Hopefully there had been some improvement since her morning ride with Matt.

First, though, she went to the barn phone to check if there was a message from Dat, but none had been left, which wasn't like Dat at all. *Mamm will worry if we don't hear something soon*, she thought, realizing she was a bit worried herself. But better her father and brother come home when it was safe than take a risk on roads that might still be treacherous in places. Somerset was nearly three hours away even in the best of conditions.

Once she and King were on their way, Liz could see that some of the Amish farmers had plowed areas of the road near their property, which was heartening.

As she rode, Liz couldn't help thinking about Matt, wondering if he'd made it home all right and how long it might be before she'd see him again. She even daydreamed about someday maybe getting to spend Christmas with him, either here or in Bird-in-Hand. To her thinking, it really didn't matter where, as long as they could celebrate together.

Tomorrow would be a reenactment of what her family had always done for as long as she could remember, a day to honor the Lord Jesus and enjoy each other's company. But if Dat and Adam weren't able to get home, things would be off-kilter. Once more Liz prayed silently that all would be well, and that God would guide them safely home. And as she went, Liz kept an eye out for a passenger van. *Just in case they make it.* Oh, she hoped so!

She also contemplated Adam's return and what it would mean for her tours but hadn't discussed her thoughts on that yet with Matt. As enthusiastic as he had been about working with her, she could only hope he might be willing to continue on. *Surely Adam would be relieved*, she thought. *He never expected to do this permanently, anyhow.*

The road was lumpy and bumpy in many places, with piles of packed snow here and there, especially where some farmers had shoveled out a ways from their driveways or lanes.

Without a rise in temperatures over the next couple days, the snowpack would remain. Even so, Liz thought that if she took it slow with the horse and buggy, she could get Mamm and Martha Rose safely to the Christmas House and back home this evening. It was a short distance, and the enclosed buggy would be warmer than riding in an open sleigh, for sure.

O Lord, please help us and any who might go to the Hyatts' place to get there safely, she prayed as she turned back toward home.

20

When it was close to their usual early suppertime and Dat and Adam still were not to be seen or heard from, Liz once more headed out to the barn to check for a voice message. She was pleased to learn as she picked up the phone that there was, indeed, a message waiting, and from Dat, no less.

"Hullo, I'm callin' from Somerset. Adam and I tried to get out early this morning, but the roads were still a mess and drifted shut in places. Hopin' to be home for supper if we can get a driver, but if not, please don't fret. Go ahead without us. We're warm and dry at my cousins' house. We'll look forward to celebrating whenever we can get there. Love to each of you."

Smiling, Liz saved the message for Mamm. *She'll be so relieved*, Liz thought, heading back to the house to let Mamm and Martha Rose know, feeling lighter herself.

At the news, Mamm decided to wait no longer to get the goulash—Dat's favorite dish—on the table. There was plenty to eat, including buttered lima beans and chow chow, so Dat and Adam could have leftovers if they arrived later on, though Dat was not one to eat much close to bedtime.

Without Dat and Adam present, there was a tangible emptiness at the meal, and Liz prayed they would soon make it home.

After supper, Mamm and Martha Rose got into the family carriage. Liz sat in front and picked up the driving lines, while Mamm and Martha Rose each held a quart jar on their blanket-covered laps. Mamm had also insisted on bringing along several knotted comforters to give, as well as two battery-operated candles.

Liz had hoped to arrive a little early at the Christmas House, so they parked on the far side, waiting. The sun had set two hours prior, but the waxing moon and the stars were brightly visible as several enclosed buggies and a few men on horseback began to arrive.

Soon, even more neighbors were coming on foot, so Liz, Mamm, and Martha Rose walked down toward the house, where Liz motioned for folks to congregate with them. Quickly, the People made a long line across the front yard, three rows deep, all of them standing silently with their canned goods, blankets, and the candles.

After a time, once the stream of new arrivals, which included Preacher Yoder and the bishop, had ceased, Liz told the first person in line, Onkel Joe, to pass down her instructions to the next one. Then she walked toward the dark, quiet house.

A good many came! she thought, delighted.

She knocked on the door and stepped back a little, holding one of the lit candles so her face could be seen.

Ashley Hyatt answered the door and immediately smiled. "Wow, Liz, this is a surprise. What brings you out on such a cold night?"

"Merry Christmas!" Liz replied, turning to point to everyone behind her—rows of Amish folk now, their candles all lit. "We noticed your power was out and wanted to help."

Ashley's eyes glimmered as she took in the crowd, nearly all of Hickory Hollow, it seemed—families and even little children. Then, slowly, she turned to call for Logan and their own children, who soon appeared wearing coats and hoods and scarves.

Logan looked stunned, eyes wide in disbelief. "What's this?" he asked as the People began to bring their canned goods of homemade chili soup and a variety of other things—baked goods, flashlights, woolen blankets, and even bundles of firewood—onto the porch.

Then, as Liz had instructed, one by one, the neighbors who had fretted and complained about the Christmas House display began to place their lit candles in the snow surrounding the large nativity scene in the side yard.

The loneliest neighbors have the biggest Christmas display, thought Liz unexpectedly as she gazed at the only visible thing in the yard—the lovely nativity. Santa, his sleigh, and the dancing elves, and everything else unrelated to the true meaning of Christmas remained dark. But the Christ child in a bed of hay shone brilliantly.

A passenger van pulled up just then, and Liz saw a young man get out and cross the road to join the People. Only when she heard his clear voice lead out in "Silent Night" did she know it was Matt. The People joined him in singing, and Ashley, now wearing a hooded wool coat and boots, reached to link arms with Liz there on the porch, blending her voice with all the others, including her husband and children.

Liz's heart warmed at seeing the big gathering and such generosity. *This is what I'm meant to do*, she thought. *See others through God's eyes . . . bring people together.*

"All is calm, all is bright." Everyone sang the well-known lyrics, and Liz couldn't keep her voice from wavering at the sight of so many candles lighting up the holy family.

Jesus, the Light of the world.

And hearing the beloved carol sung so sweetly by young and old alike gave her hope that this moment might be the start of a new beginning in the hollow.

"You're amazing, Liz," Ashley said, standing shoulder to shoulder with her. "Merry Christmas to you and your family."

"Thank you, *everyone*!" Logan said loudly. Then, observing the candlelit nativity, he added, "I've decided that this nativity will be the focal point of my Christmas decorating in the future." He paused before adding, "Although I might have to include a Bethlehem star, three kings, and a few more shepherds and sheep."

Spontaneous applause broke out, as well as a few chuckles.

"I also want to apologize for the unintended repercussions this enormous holiday display has had for many of you." Here, he shook his head. "I only wanted to share the Christmas spirit. But you've shown me that coming together to help others is a way *all* of us can enjoy celebrating."

Bishop Beiler moved out of the crowd just then and walked up to the porch to give Logan a firm handshake, then stood there with him in solidarity.

Many of the Amish waved before turning to head back to their horses and buggies, some still humming "Silent Night" as they went.

To Liz's delight, Matt was waiting at the end of the walkway, so she headed there, leaving Mamm and Martha Rose on the porch to talk with Ashley and pet Kippy Sue, whose tail thumped against the floor as if she was delighted by all the attention. Liz was touched to see Matt sporting his new navy-blue knit hat and the scarf she'd made.

"What a *wunnerbaar-gut* idea, Lizzy. I just had to come and see this for myself," he said softly.

She smiled. "I'm so glad."

"Does the offer for hot cocoa still stand?" he asked.

"How 'bout tonight?"

"Invitation accepted."

Her heart filled with delight at the prospect of spending more time with him.

Just then, she heard what sounded like her father's voice. *Could it be?*

And there, amongst the last few neighbors milling about, were Dat and Adam, walking in their direction.

"Oh, *mei Lieb*!" Mamm said at the sight of Dat and hurried down the front walkway.

Dat wrapped a big arm around her shoulders. "I'm so happy to see ya," he said. "Our driver seemed to know just where we could find ya." He motioned for the van to pull up closer.

Mamm's face was beaming as tears welled up. "Merry Christmas," she whispered. "You're almost home."

"*Nee*, I'm home *now*." He smiled and suggested that Mamm and Martha Rose ride with him and Adam in the warm van to the house. "Matt and Liz can follow in the buggy," Dat said, grinning at Matt knowingly as though taking credit for their being together. "Your Mamm's been keepin' me in the loop."

Liz couldn't help smiling all the way to the waiting horse and buggy.

"Mind if I take the reins?" Matt asked her.

"Not at all," she said. "I've got a perty *gut* idea of your drivin' skills."

Matt's laughter rang out into the chill air, the sound of it warming Liz's heart.

"I wonder how Dat and Adam knew 'bout the Christmas House gathering tonight," Liz said when they were on their way. "I mean, have ya ever known the Amish grapevine to spread news that far so quick?"

Matt was chuckling. "Well, we came in the same van, interestingly enough. Bill stopped in Bird-in-Hand on the way from Somerset to pick me up."

Liz couldn't believe it. "What're the chances of that?"

"Well, Lizzy . . . it's nearly Christmas." He moved both reins to his right hand and reached for her hand with the other. "The Lord has His own perfect way of answerin' prayers."

She smiled again in agreement. "There's been a lot of prayin', for certain."

At the house, Matt halted the horse over near the stable, where Dat must have hung a lantern since the sky was so dark. Still sitting in the carriage with her, Matt pulled something out of his coat pocket. "This is for you, Lizzy." He gave her a flat, wrapped box.

Curious, she opened it to see a pair of ladies' black leather gloves in the dim light. "It's the ideal gift for the winter tours ahead." She tried them on, pleased. "*Denki*, Matt." She paused a moment, thinking about what she truly wanted to say. "I hope ya might be along for those tours, too."

Matt studied her in the lantern's light. "If that's what ya want, I'll be there." He paused a moment. "I'd really like to spend as much time as possible with the woman I hope to court."

Oh, she loved hearing this, with all of her heart. "Maybe at some point the tours can expand to more carriages and drivers," she ventured.

"I like how you're thinkin'." He was grinning now. "And what if we grew the buggy business . . . together?" He reached for her gloved hand and raised it to his lips. "Remember, we're a team, Lizzy."

She smiled back at him. They were indeed.

Her heart soared with joy on this very special night.

Peppermint Taffy

Note from Bev

Lots of fun to make and to eat. Try this recipe once, and a quaint and happy Christmas tradition may await you, just as has been enjoyed by the many Amish folk who make taffy together as a family during the holidays and beyond.

1 tablespoon unflavored gelatin
½ cup cold water
2 pounds granulated sugar
2 cups cream
2 cups light corn syrup
1½ to 2 teaspoons peppermint extract
Paraffin wax (size of a walnut)

Soak gelatin in cold water. Boil sugar, cream, corn syrup, peppermint extract, and paraffin wax for 15 minutes; stir in gelatin and boil until a tiny bit of the mixture put in cold water hardens immediately (hard-ball test).

Let cool. Pull taffy in a cool place, buttering hands slightly so taffy will not stick to them. Stretch the mixture out 12 inches or more and fold it over itself again and again for 10 to 15 minutes until it is glossy and light in color. The taffy will turn from translucent to opaque.

---

*This is a variation of the taffy recipe in *The Beverly Lewis Amish Heritage Cookbook, 20th Anniversary Edition*. Available now wherever books are sold.

Chocolate Christmas Cookies

Cookies:

4 cups flour
1 teaspoon baking soda
½ teaspoon salt
1 cup butter, softened
2 cups light brown sugar
2 eggs
2 teaspoons instant coffee granules
¾ cup baking cocoa
¼ cup olive oil
1⅓ cups sour cream
2 cups angel flake coconut
2 cups English walnuts, chopped

Icing:

6 tablespoons baking cocoa
2 tablespoons olive oil
½ cup sour cream
½ cup butter, softened
4 cups confectioners' sugar

Heat oven to 350°F.

Cookies:

Mix together flour, baking soda, and salt; set aside.

Beat together butter, sugar, eggs, coffee, cocoa, olive oil, and sour cream. Gradually stir in the dry ingredients. Add coconut and walnuts; mix well.

Drop by tablespoons onto greased baking sheets; bake at 350°F for 10 minutes. Cool.

Icing:

Mix together cocoa, olive oil, sour cream, and butter. Stir in confectioners' sugar until desired consistency is reached. Spread icing on cookies once they are completely cool.

---

*Recipe taken from p. 196 of *The Beverly Lewis Amish Heritage Cookbook, 20th Anniversary Edition*. Available now wherever books are sold.

Discussion Questions

1. Liz's business, Amish Buggy Rides, offers a wide variety of tours—the Amish Back Roads and Tasty Treats Tour, the Amish Farm Tour, the Christmas House Buggy Tour . . . Which tour would you book if you were heading to Hickory Hollow?
2. Although it's a bit unorthodox within her community, Liz's drive to start her own business turned Amish Buggy Rides into a highlight for local tourists. If you could open any business of your own, what would it be?
3. Early in the book, we come to learn that "The Christmas House" is the name given to the Hyatt family's residence and the elaborate light display in their yard. How did your feelings toward the Hyatts and their splashy décor change throughout the story?
4. Ella Mae serves her community by providing a listening ear, impartial perspective, prayers, and her trademark peppermint tea to those who visit her. Who is the "Ella Mae" in your life?
5. Through Liz's story, readers are shown how Christmas is

celebrated in Amish communities. Some traditions may reflect those of Englishers (non-Amish individuals)—gathering with family, baking, exchanging gifts—while others, such as a minimalistic approach to Christmas decorations, may be unfamiliar. What details surprised you?

6. During one of her buggy tours, Liz admires the beauty of Hickory Hollow through the fresh eyes of her passengers and asks herself, "Do I take these everyday scenes for granted? There's so much to love about life here" (page 104). It's not uncommon for us to lose sight of the beauty in what's become familiar. What are some of the beauties that have become routine or commonplace in your own life?
7. Food is something that brings people together over the holidays, and families often have traditions that revolve around making seasonal favorites with one another. One of the Lantz family's Christmas traditions is making homemade peppermint taffy. What are some of the holiday treats and traditions in your own family?
8. Throughout the story, readers see Liz's passion for "shining God's light to others, even in the small ways" (page 47), whether it's through her interactions with her customers or shifting her community's perspective on the ostracized Hyatt family. What are small ways we can incorporate this type of mindset into our daily lives? When has someone—even a stranger—shown you God's light in a small way?

Author's Note

Oh, Christmas! My favorite holiday, when family traditions bring significant meaning and beauty to the celebration of Christ's birth.

Even though our three children are grown, I still hang their quilted snow-white Christmas stockings on the mantel and tuck sweet little cards and other special tokens of love inside to be opened on Christmas Day. I also decorate several trees in the house with my husband's help and endearing humor. And like my Amish friends do, I string up cards in the breakfast nook and bake cherry pies, snickerdoodles, and chocolate Christmas cookies.

I also enjoy seeing the Christmas lights while driving around town with our family, all of us singing carols in four-part harmony. Dave maps out the route beforehand, choosing the most elaborately decorated homes—the top twenty as listed in the local news—some displays with synchronized music like Logan Hyatt's Christmas House.

Most inspiring, though, is the candlelight church service, especially the tender moment when the congregation sings

"Silent night, holy night" and raises hundreds of candles in honor of the babe in the manger. My tears well up as my family stands there with me, and once again I breathe a prayer of immense gratitude to God for sending Jesus to offer hope and eternal life to this fallen world.

My best wishes for the season are filled with joy for you as you gather with family and friends to rejoice in the birthday of our Savior—God's most precious Gift for you, and for me.

BEVERLY LEWIS, born in the heart of Pennsylvania Dutch country, has sold more than 19 million books. Her stories have been published in twelve languages and have regularly appeared on numerous bestseller lists, including *The New York Times* and *USA Today*. A keen interest in her mother's Plain heritage has inspired Beverly to write many Amish-related novels, beginning with *The Shunning*, which has sold more than one million copies and is an Original Hallmark Channel movie, along with its sequels, *The Confession* and *The Reckoning*. In 2007, *The Brethren* was honored with a Christy Award.

Beverly has been interviewed by both national and international media, including *Time* magazine, the Associated Press, and the BBC. She lives with her husband, David, in Colorado, where they enjoy hiking, making music, and spending time with their family.

Visit her website at BeverlyLewis.com or Facebook.com/OfficialBeverlyLewis for more information.

The Beverly Lewis Amish Heritage Cookbook

20th Anniversary Edition

More than 200 favorite, time-tested recipes collected and passed down by Beverly Lewis from Amish and Plain family and friends and updated for the benefit of cooks with less time to spend in the kitchen. Perfect for gift giving, this updated volume also contains a new foreword, as well as a trove of Amish sayings, household tips, story excerpts, and personal glimpses from beloved bestselling author Beverly Lewis.

Sign Up for Beverly's Newsletter

Keep up to date with Beverly's latest news on book releases and events by signing up for her email list at the link below.

FOLLOW BEVERLY ON SOCIAL MEDIA

Beverly Lewis

BeverlyLewis.com